A MATCH MADE

IN DOG TOWN

SANDY RIDEOUT

ELLEN RIGGS

FREE PREQUEL

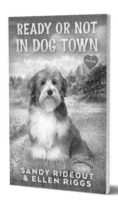

A Rescue Dog and an Unexpected Date with Destiny

Meet Isla McInnis, a reporter who flies across the country to Dorset Hills on a hunch that a sweet little rescue dog named Rio will change her life forever. A quirky band of rescue rebels shows her the true reason she was called to this quaint town in the first place. Join Sandy Rideout's author newsletter at **Sandyrideout.com** to get the FREE PREQUEL to the Dog Town cozy-romance series at sandyrideout.com.

A Match Made in Dog Town

Copyright © 2018 Sandy Rideout

ISBN 978-1-9994313-1-0 eBook
ISBN 978-1-9994313-3-4 Book
ASIN B07FZRSY4S Kindle
ASIN 1999431332 Paperback

Publisher: Sandy Rideout
www.sandyrideout.com
Cover designer: Lou Harper
Editor: Serena Clarke
2103081341

CONTENTS

WELCOME TO DOG TOWN!

Dear Reader,

I used to be a diehard cat lady. Then I got my first dog ever and I was a goner! A journalist by training, I interviewed every expert I could find: trainers, breeders, groomers, walkers and more. The journey ultimately brought me here, to Dog Town.

Dorset Hills, better known as *Dog Town*, is famous for being the most dog-friendly place in the world. People come from near and far to enjoy its beautiful landscape and unique charms. Naturally, when so many dogs and dog-lovers unite in one town, mischief and mayhem ensue.

In the Dog Town cozy-romance series, you can expect the humor, the quirky, loveable characters and the edge-of-your-seat suspense that are part of any cozy mystery, but there's a little more romance and a lot less murder. In fact, *no one dies!* I can guarantee you'll laugh out loud and enjoy hair-raising adventures, heartwarming holidays and happily-ever-afters for both humans and pets.

You can read the books in any order, but it's more fun to work your way through the seasons in Dog Town:

- *Ready or Not in Dog Town* (The Beginning)
- *Bitter and Sweet in Dog Town* (Labor Day)
- *A Match Made in Dog Town* (Thanksgiving)

- *Lost and Found in Dog Town* (Christmas)
- *Calm and Bright in Dog Town* (Christmas)
- *Tried and True in Dog Town* (New Year's)
- *Yours and Mine in Dog Town* (Valentine's Day)
- *Nine Lives in Dog Town* (Easter)
- *Great and Small in Dog Town* (Memorial Day)
- *Bold and Blue in Dog Town* (Independence Day)
- *Better or Worse in Dog Town* (Labor Day)

If you fancy more murder with your mystery, be sure to join my newsletter to get the FREE PREQUEL to the Bought-the-Farm Cozy Mystery series. My newsletter is filled with funny stories and photos of my adorable dogs. Don't miss out!

Take care,
Sandy (and Ellen)

CHAPTER ONE

D orset Hills was a very pretty town that had never made the mistake of taking its good looks for granted. Even in autumn, when the famous hills were aflame with glorious color, residents worked hard to keep up appearances. It had been a stroke of great luck that a national magazine named Dorset Hills the best place in North America for dogs and dog-lovers. The town had grown into a small city on the strength of that title. But no one rested on their laurels in Dorset Hills, more affectionately known as "Dog Town." There were always other pretty towns waiting to nip at their heels. It was important to keep on hustling.

Holidays offered the perfect opportunity to showcase both the city's natural gifts and its quirky charm. A political subcommittee met regularly to plan seasonal decorations, activities and marketing. Although no occasion was too small to celebrate, city staff pulled out all the stops in the weeks before Hallowe'en and built toward a spectacular finale at Christmas. It took stamina to deliver on all the festivities, but it was a pleasure as well as a duty.

Dorset Hills smiled upon anyone who made the city

look good. Bridget Linsmore was one of those people. For nearly 10 years she'd hosted the Thanksgiving Rescue Dog Pageant, which had become a popular event on the Dorset Hills social calendar. The fundraiser brought tourists from all over Hills country and filled the coffers for Bridget's rescue program.

Despite her contributions to Dorset Hills, however, Bridget always raised a few eyebrows when she drove through town in her old lime-green van bursting with lovable mutts. Even in a city that built its reputation on dogs, some said that a woman could simply have too many. Bridget's jacket was usually covered in dog hair and slobber, and her boots caked in mud. As for her hair... well, the less said the better. Not that a few stares bothered Bridget. Unlike many in Dog Town, Bridget cared little about appearances. She had enough on her mind, particularly as the countdown to the pageant began.

Just after two o'clock on Friday, November first, Bridget pulled into a parking spot on Main Street behind a white truck bearing the City's crest. Staff in regulation coveralls were on ladders replacing Hallowe'en decorations with Thanksgiving garlands on the old-fashioned iron lampposts. There were no miniature gourds in the wreaths this year. City Council had quietly banned them after youths raided the town's displays and pelted Main Street's quaint store-fronts. A tasteful presentation was central to the Dorset Hills brand, and exploded squash sent the wrong message.

Opening the rear door of the van, Bridget released seven dogs of various sizes, breeds and colors. As she strode along Main Street, enjoying the crisp air and sunshine, the dogs fanned out like a flock of geese behind Beau, Bridget's lead dog and constant companion. Pedestrians moved aside to avoid tripping over the big dogs or kicking the little ones.

When she got to the Lucky Dog Barkery, she raised her right hand, palm up. Seven furry backsides went down. Seven pairs of eager eyes rose to meet hers.

"Looks like a good crop this year," an old man said, smiling.

"All dogs are good," Bridget said. "People not so much."

The man laughed. Few took offence at her brusque manner. Her intentions were kind, and no one doubted that for a second.

Bridget was Dorset Hills' matchmaker to the dogs. She had an unerring instinct for placing the right rescue dog with the right owner—and sometimes pairing happy humans, too. She wasn't overly sentimental about it. Bringing dogs and dog-lovers together had always come naturally to her. Now it was business, and she worked hard to stay detached.

After picking up kibble and other supplies, she headed back to the van. Just as she slid behind the wheel, her phone rang. "Yeah?"

"Yeah? That's how you greet your best friend?"

Bridget grinned. "Hey, Duff."

The nickname didn't particularly suit Andrea MacDuff, but it had stuck. "Why so surly?" she asked.

"Surly is my default state. You know me, right?"

"I know there's a heart of gold under that crusty old jacket," Duff said.

Glancing down, Bridget brushed away dog hairs before rapping her knuckles against her chest. "Wrong. Hollow."

"Really? Well, maybe we'll find your heart down in Wychwood Grove. There's a house I want you to see."

Bridget stopped scraping at a mystery stain. "A house?"

"I'll send you the address and you can meet me there."

"Now? But I—"

"Property doesn't last long around here, Bee. Even a place that needs a lot of work."

Beau pushed his head under Bridget's hand and she stroked his ears. "So, you're saying it's a dump?"

Duff laughed. "A diamond in the rough. Still, it'll go fast. I had to use my considerable charms to get an early viewing. The listing goes live tomorrow."

She wasn't exaggerating about her charms. Duff had all the polish Bridget lacked, and it served her well as one of Dorset Hills' up-and-coming real estate agents.

Bridget shook her head. "I'm not ready to buy, Duff."

"No one's ever ready for her first house or her first baby."

"And you'd know that *how*?"

Despite her career success, Duff chose to rent an apartment over a shop that sold doll houses. She liked the irony, and besides, she saw too many great properties to settle on just one. Her dream house was always just around the corner, just like the perfect man.

"I've midwifed tons of first home purchases, that's how. Buckle up, my friend."

Bridget reluctantly snapped on her seatbelt. She hated feeling constrained but she couldn't afford any more tickets. "The timing's terrible. I've got too much to do without buying a house on top of it."

"No one should buy the first house they see, anyway. But you've got to start somewhere to have a baseline."

"Can't we do that after the pageant?"

A passerby rapped on the van's window to say hello and regretted it when the dogs started barking. Duff waited for the noise to die down before continuing. "Hardly anyone lists in winter, Bee. We'd better dive in today."

Bridget flipped the wipers to clear the windshield. Dust

had drifted down from the wheat woven into the wreaths installed overhead. The City was always trying something new and different, but it seemed unlikely that wheat would go the distance.

"But what if I actually like this dump?" she asked.

"You won't. You'll be appalled. Then everything else will look good."

"Again, do you know me?" Bridget laughed. "Fixer-uppers are my type."

"In dogs, not houses. Anyway, this will take an hour, tops. So, drop off the dogs and come meet me."

Bridget glanced at Beau in the passenger seat. He was a tall, black dog with the grace of a poodle and the silky feathers of an Irish setter. Even as a puppy he'd been chill, and he'd matured into the most self-possessed dog Bridget had ever known—and she'd known a lot of them. "What do you think, fella?"

Beau gently placed his paw over Bridget's hand on the stick shift.

"What's the verdict?" Duff's voice sounded distant, as if she had her head stuck out her car window.

"You're so sure I'll say yes that you're halfway there already. And you're having a smoke to calm your nerves."

Duff gave a self-conscious cough. "I don't smoke."

"If you lie to me about that, how can I believe what you tell me about this dump of a house?"

"Okay, I rarely smoke, and only when I'm nervous."

Bridget turned the key in the ignition but stayed where she was. "Why are you nervous about this junker I shouldn't buy?"

There was a long pause as Duff took a last, loving drag. "Because I want you to have a house, Bee. You've busted your butt rehabbing dogs for ten years. You've made tons of people happy and sent them off with the right dog and even the right partner. It's your turn to be happy. You need a house to expand."

"I'm not unhappy." Bridget scratched Beau's ears thoughtfully. "But I do hate having to turn away rescue dogs because I don't have space. It keeps me up at night sometimes."

"See? It's time. Just check this place out."

Finally, Bridget pulled into the traffic on Main Street. "Let me think. I'll call you in ten minutes, okay?"

She dropped the phone before Duff could answer and ignored the instant buzzing of texts. Driving through downtown traffic took her full attention anyway. There was always a jam outside City Hall, worse on nice days when the sun bounced off the gold limestone and made it gleam like a fairy-tale castle.

To escape the crush, Bridget turned north at the Barton Gallery of Art, with its twin bronze wolfhound statues flanking the front entrance. The route was no better, because drivers had slowed down to take in the breathtaking view of the hills. Taking a left, she headed west at a snail's pace. If she wanted to get to Wychwood Grove before Duff combusted, she'd have to get creative.

Turning south, she headed toward the water, where traffic tended to be lighter. Lake Longmuir was little more than a wide, shallow pond but the streams running down from the hills kept it fresh and clear most of the year. The boardwalk along the lakefront was crowded with pedestrians and dogs, however, and Bridget realized her mistake. Nothing caused more rubbernecking in Dorset Hills than dogs on parade.

"Oh, Beau, people are idiots." She turned right and then left again at Dorset Hills General Hospital. Outside sat a hulking bronze St. Bernard dog, complete with rescue cask attached to its collar. A local artist was making a killing casting these eight-foot-tall statues for the main institutions in the city. The City funded some of them; others were donated by wealthy patrons. The bronze dogs had caught on like wildfire with visitors. They took the bus tour, posed with the statues, and shared the photos on social media to win prizes.

Bridget liked the bronze collection although she thought the money could have been better spent on animal services. Plus, it irked her to no end that the statues were all purebreds. She spent her life surrounded by adorable mutts of indeterminate origins. Highlighting purebreds sent the wrong message. An elitist message.

Another turn at the Dalmatian outside the fire hall took her into Riverdale. The neighborhood that had once featured small cottages was gradually being not only gentrified but also homogenized. Dorset Hills favored graceful grey two-story houses with black accents. Bridget's rusty van didn't fit in with the fancy cars sitting in driveways now.

Pulling up to a drab bungalow, she hopped out and released the dogs. Following them into the back yard, she yanked poop bags out of her pocket and stooped to scoop. She worked hard to keep the place tidy. If the dogs had their way, the lawn would be a lunar landscape. Fritz, a shaggy gray-and-white terrier mix, barked to let people know he was back and Bridget silenced him promptly. She was careful to avoid giving the neighbors cause to complain.

Six other dogs waited inside, tails lashing and tongues lolling. There were 13, including Beau, but they were a civilized crew. With only weeks left till the pageant, their training was nearly complete. Soon, all but Beau would move on, and new dogs would gradually join them as the cycle repeated.

Opening the front door, Bridget reached into the mailbox. There was a small envelope with her name on it in her landlady's elaborate script. She tore it open and pulled out a pretty card with kittens in a basket on the front.

"Dear Bridget: My niece is moving back to Dorset Hills and I'd love to offer this house to her. I'm wondering if you might have plans to move. Not till after the pageant, of course. But before Christmas would be wonderful. I know this year's pageant is going to be a smash hit! Let me know your plans, dear. All the best, Mrs. Lenderwurst."

Bridget's hand shook as she set the card on the kitchen table. Beau stuck close to her side as she began to pace. His tail hung straight down, feathers nearly brushing the floor.

"It's okay, buddy," she said. "She's not evicting us. She can't. We haven't done anything wrong."

The other dogs had piled onto the shabby couch or collapsed onto the dog beds scattered around the living room. The floor was bare and the curtains looped up out of reach. Bridget had never bothered to decorate, partly because of the dogs but mostly because living here was never meant to be permanent. It had been the perfect place to land when she'd finished college and come back to Dorset Hills with a useless degree in anthropology. At first there had been roommates; as they'd left, she'd replaced them with more and more dogs.

The sun cast weak rays over the stark room, and Bridget suddenly realized this place had never felt like home. There was no reason to cling to it, especially if she wasn't welcome.

Picking up her phone, she texted Duff: "Let's see if your ugly duckling is my swan."

CHAPTER TWO

Bridget wondered if she was the first person to fall in love with a driveway. It was long and curvy, with squat trees on either side that would flower in spring. Behind them were towering maples that shook rusty orange leaves onto the well-packed gravel. At the bottom, massive twin oak trees the color of oxblood stood sentinel where the drive opened to a parking area large enough to hold at least 15 cars. The house itself was a sprawling cottage, with smoke drifting up from the chimney. It was painted the mild blue of a summer afternoon's sky. In Wychwood Grove, houses were often colorful—red, orange, yellow, teal and even pink. It was a like a maritime harbor, only without the sea. No doubt City Council would crack down on that eventually and issue an order to neutralize to match the downtown core.

Duff was standing beside her red SUV, grinding something into the gravel with one stiletto-heeled boot. She was dressed impeccably in a black wool coat with a silk scarf that matched her blue eyes. Her hair grazed her shoulders in a sleek auburn bob. Redheads were wise to keep it simple, she always said. She stood out in any crowd as it was.

Beau jumped out of the van after Bridget, and Duff's wide smile downgraded to a thin line. "You can't bring a dog to a house showing, Bee."

"Beau's not a dog, per se," Bridget said, as he took his habitual position at her left side.

"Newsflash... he's a dog. And a large, imposing one at that."

"He's my quality control manager. What he doesn't like, I don't like."

Duff rolled her eyes. "The owners are home, so he can't come inside unless they give permission."

"It's Dog Town, Duff. I doubt they'll be shocked." Bridget followed her friend around the house and into the backyard, where the earth was spongy and covered in damp leaves. It smelled like mold and fungus and all the good things of cottage life. "How can you walk in those things?"

Stepping lightly over slippery slabs of shale, Duff laughed. "I can leap tall buildings in a single bound in heels. I feel the same way about them as you feel about Beau."

Bridget rested her right hand on Beau's sleek head. "I doubt that."

They crossed a stretch of lawn and then followed a short path of cedar chips through a thatch of young, gold maples. Finally, Duff stopped, and raised her arms dramatically. "Voila."

The sound that came out Bridget's mouth was half-gasp, half-groan. "No!"

"Yes. Yes, my friend." Duff's huge grin swallowed most of the freckles that dusted her cheeks.

Before them sat an old red barn. There were few barns left in Dorset Hills that hadn't been converted to posh artist lofts. Through the double front door, Bridget glimpsed several antique cars, most covered in drop sheets.

"I want it," Bridget said. "Mine, Duffy. Mine mine mine."

"The barn would make a great kennel and let you expand. But it needs some work, Bee. And the house, too."

Bridget blinked a few times, afraid the image would vanish. Then she rubbed her eyes, which were the gray-green of the lichen on the barn's wall. "It's gorgeous."

Duff laughed. "Oh, Bee, only you could see beauty in a rickety old barn."

Bridget laughed, too, and Beau joined them, his tail going around like a propeller. "I see what it could be, given some love and grooming."

"Remember what I said: lots of people fall for the first house they tour, but that doesn't mean it's the best one. Just keep an open mind, okay?"

They walked through the barn, and Bridget spun around to view it from every angle. It wasn't a complete wreck, but the floor sagged in places and heavy dampness hinted at leaks above.

When Duff finally lured Bridget back outside, a silver-haired man was pulling logs from a woodpile and dropping them into a wheelbarrow.

"Well, hello," he said, smiling at Bridget. "I know you, young lady. You matched my daughter, Stacey, to her husband."

"Stacey Olson, yes!" Bridget beamed at him. "Actually, I matched your daughter to a Doberman mutt named Peanut. The husband was just a lucky accident."

He selected another log from the pile. "Speaking of accidents, they're expecting twins any day. My wife and I want to move closer and help out."

"Ah, so that's why you're selling this beautiful place," Bridget said. "I couldn't understand why anyone would let it go."

Standing behind Mr. Olson, Duff pressed her finger to her lips. Prospective buyers were probably supposed to play harder to get.

The old man sighed. "This house has so many wonderful family memories. But it's getting harder for me to keep up with everything." He ran a gloved hand over the logs. "I'm proud of this woodpile, but it takes work."

"I can see that," Bridget said, admiring the stacked, even rows.

Beau nudged Mr. Olson's hand, and he automatically stroked the dog's shoulder. "Now that is a beautiful animal. Is he one of your rescues?"

"Once upon a time, yes. Now he's the love of my life."

Mr. Olson shook his head. "Pretty girl like you needs more than dogs."

"Dogs are less trouble. Even thirteen of them."

"My wife would probably agree with you," he said, with a chuckle. "Come inside and meet her. The dog is more than welcome."

Bridget made a face at Duff, who rolled her eyes again.

After they greeted Mrs. Olson and downed a quick cup of tea, Duff led Bridget around the house quietly pointing out every fault and flaw. Bridget countered each negative comment. The cramped third floor bedroom with the sloped ceilings would make a perfect office, she said, and the dingy laundry room was better than the non-existent one she had now. The dated kitchen had charm, and the powder room was so small it would be easy to clean.

Duff stared at her. "Are you stoned, Bridget? I've never heard you like this. You're... *bubbly*."

"Bubbly? Ridiculous." Looking around the kitchen, she pulled a long breath in through her nose. "They must be piping something into the air."

Perching on a hoop-backed chair at the kitchen table, Duff persisted. "Is there something you're not telling me, Bee?"

Bridget pulled the card with the kittens out of her purse and handed it to Duff. "My landlady wants me out by Christmas."

"She can't evict you unless she's moving in herself. That's the law. You can make her prove it to the City."

"I know, but it's awful. I've been a good tenant for 12 years. You know how much of my own money I've put into keeping the place up."

"You're an excellent tenant and she's lucky to have you," Duff said.

Beau pressed against Bridget, sensing her concern. "Who else would rent to me? Everyone knows about my rescue program."

"Still, you can't buy this house just because your landlady's making empty threats. It has to be a considered decision."

"Well, let's consider it, then."

Together, they flipped through the home inspection the owners had commissioned early, in hopes of creating a bidding war when the listing went live the next day. Real estate in Dorset Hills had spiraled out of control in the past five years. Even here on the fringes, houses sold for way over asking price.

Duff tapped a polished maroon nail on every issue cited, murmuring disapproval. The Olsons hadn't kept up the house as well as they could have, and the inspection had a long list of required repairs, some more urgent than others.

"The roof needs to be replaced," Duff said. "That's at least ten grand. And the porch is unstable, which is another three. The plumbing isn't up to grade, either."

Bridget deflated with every tap of Duff's fingernail. Fighting tears, she said, "I guess you're right. It's hopeless."

"Hopeless? I never said that. All of those things can be fixed if you really want the house. But we'd need to get it for the right price to leave a budget for repairs."

"Do I have enough now? I was counting on the pageant to build my down payment."

Duff rested her chin on clasped hands. "Honestly, Bee, I doubt it. I think they'll get multiple offers. If you go in too high, the roof won't get done."

Running her hand along white wainscoting, Bridget nodded. "Okay. I understand."

After a moment's hesitation, Duff touched her friend's arm. "Do you think your mom might help out?"

Bridget jerked her arm away. "I'm not asking my mom for money. You know how much she hates Dorset Hills."

"Okay, okay. Forget I mentioned it."

"I know you like her, Duff, but trust me when I say that wears off when you get to know her better."

Bridget and her mom had grated on each other through years of crisscrossing the country for her father's job. When he'd passed away three years earlier, Bridget had been devastated, whereas her mom had dusted herself off quickly and settled just far enough away that they had a good excuse not to visit each other.

Duff closed the inspection binder. "Why don't we chat later when you've had some time to think? We can make an offer tomorrow if you want."

Taking a last look around, Bridget led the way out to the van in silence. She opened the driver's door and Beau jumped through to the passenger seat. Then she slid behind the wheel and rolled down the window. "I guess you're right. I should wait for a house that doesn't break my bank."

There was a pinging sound of gravel on metal, and they both looked up the driveway. A low silver sports car was practically flying toward them, sending bright leaves twirling up in tiny tornados.

Duff turned as the tiny convertible reversed into the spot beside her car. Bridget peered around her. The car looked freshly washed and sparkled in the now-setting sun. The driver didn't own a dog, of that she was sure.

The car door opened and a dark-haired man unfolded from it. He was surprisingly tall and broad-shouldered given the size of the car. Pulling off his shades, he dropped them on the seat before closing the door and heading toward the house. He didn't even look their way.

"Wow," Duffy said. "What is that?"

The man's gait was elegant and effortless. On a driveway thick with dust he didn't raise a cloud. "A vampire?" Bridget guessed. "Or a shapeshifter? He's a luxury car in human form."

"That he is." Duff's hand twitched, as if she wanted to fan herself.

After knocking on the front door, the guy finally turned and glanced toward them.

"Wait, I know that guy," Bridget said, ducking. "I turned him down two years ago."

"For a date?"

"No, not a date. When's the last time I went on a date?"

"Too long ago to remember. You should do something about that."

"What's he doing here?" Bridget gasped as she realized. "Duff, get in here."

Duff came around the van and climbed into the passenger seat, shooing Beau into the back. "What gives?"

"That's the developer behind the condo going up by the lake."

The door to the house had opened and Mr. Olson was shaking the man's hand. "You mean Sullivan Shaw?"

Bridget sniffed. "Who needs two last names? It's pretentious."

"You didn't tell me Sullivan Shaw wanted one of your dogs."

"He wasn't a good fit."

"That guy is a good fit for anything."

"If he had his way, all the character would be sucked out of Dorset Hills and we'd all be living in sterile gray boxes."

Duff shook her head, bemused. "You turned him down for a dog because he follows the City's guidelines on architecture?"

"I turned him down because he's not a dog person."

"Maybe he wanted to become a dog person."

"You don't become a dog person. You either are or you aren't. And I can always tell."

Duff's phone buzzed in her hand. "Uh-oh. The Olsons' agent says they've just received a bully offer. It must be from Sullivan Shaw."

"No!" Bridget grabbed Duff's arm and shook it like a dog toy. "Mr. Slick is not knocking down my house and building a McMansion. *Do something.*"

CHAPTER THREE

"Bee, you can't buy a house just to keep someone else from having it," Duff said. "In fact, that's probably the number one reason *not* to buy a house."

"It'll break Mr. Olson's heart if Mr. Slick bulldozes all his memories. Make the offer."

Duff's fingers flew on her phone, and then paused. "You're sure, Bee? We have to go in at the top of your range."

"The pageant will probably double what it brought in last year."

"It's never a good idea to bank on what you don't have in your pocket already. I hate to sound negative, Bee. As your agent, I'm sure it will be fine. As your friend, I worry."

"Just give me a second to think." Bridget took a few deep breaths, turning to scan as much of the property as she could see from the car. Beau licked her cheek. His tail fanned gently and steadily back and forth. "Okay. Do it."

Hitting 'send,' Duff leaned back against the headrest and closed her eyes. "If it's meant to be, it'll be. Mr. Slick is likely to counter your offer, and he obviously has coin to spare."

Shrugging, Bridget said, "He can try, but this house is mine. I feel it in my bones."

Duff gave her musical laugh—the one that had men dropping like flies, if they hadn't succumbed to her blue eyes already. "If it is, then you deserve it."

"I don't know about 'deserve.'" Bridget combed her unruly blonde hair with her fingers, twisted it into a knot and secured it with an elastic band. "But I can't grow where I am. And I hate feeling unwelcome there."

"You'll love having your own place. It's what you've always wanted."

It was true. Bridget had lived in so many places that she craved roots. Her heart had been broken over and over from leaving homes she liked and family dogs she loved. At least those losses had toughened her up for her work now, she thought. Every year, she managed to give up dogs she adored and go on to love new ones.

The phone buzzed and Duff's lips pressed in a thin line as she read the text. "He counter offered. It's a lot more, Bee. Thirty grand more."

"Thirty! Crap. Even if the bank said yes, I'd have zero for renovations. In my wildest dreams I'd clear that much from the pageant."

Duff patted her friend's arm. "You'll probably clear that, but do you want to stretch yourself so thin? You might have to take more shifts at the bistro."

Bridget flipped through the photos she'd taken of the Olsons' house and barn. Resting his head on her shoulder, Beau appeared to be examining them, too. He'd love having a bigger place, she knew. While he tolerated the rescue dogs, he was happy when they left and he had her all to himself. If she had a nice kennel space the house wouldn't be so crowded.

"Duff, how many places in Dorset Hills will have capacity for a kennel? I mean, honestly."

"I'm always honest with you. Except about smoking." Duff grinned. "Plenty have room for that, but I've heard the City is getting stingy with permits for new builds. So we need to find a place that already has a barn or outbuilding that can simply be refurbished. I won't say there's a lot, but they do come up."

Bridget found a contact on her phone and called her bank. With a few minutes of pleasant negotiation, they expanded her pre-approved mortgage by fifty thousand. Duff's smile fled as she sent in the new offer.

As they waited for a response, Sullivan Shaw came out of the house and walked back to his car. He was staring at Bridget's van.

"Look down, look down," Duff said, and they sunk in their seats, giggling.

"Why do we need to hide?" Bridget asked, rolling up the window.

"Because if he knows it's you—the woman who spurned him for a dog—his pride might make him bid more than this house really deserves. Why'd you turn him down, anyway?"

"He's fake, that's why."

"We're all fake, my friend. Even you."

"I am not fake."

"I will grant that you are less fake than most people. But I could point out a few—"

"Don't bother. We're hiding like teenagers spying on a rock star. I concede your point."

Duff didn't give up. "He seems like a good candidate for a dog."

Bridget shrugged, as much as she could, crumpled up. "He's arrogant, and I figured he was trying to use the rescue dog angle to fast-track his assimilation into Dorset Hills. For business, in other words."

"It doesn't mean he'd make a bad owner, necessarily."

"He could find a dog anywhere. But then he'd have to do the hard work of raising and training it himself. And guess what? Two years later, he still hasn't done it, judging by that car. It's only big enough for a teacup dog, and that wouldn't suit his image."

"You're such a snob, Bridget. If I wanted a dog, I'd want a 'turnkey,' too. I have a busy life. Does it make me a bad person for wanting an easy, trained dog?"

"Debatable." Bridget grinned to soften the blow.

"Excuse me?"

"Wanting a turnkey dog doesn't make someone a bad person. But I only have so many I can polish like gems. Demand exceeds supply, so I can be super selective about where they go."

The phone buzzed again, and this time, Duff's jaw clenched. "He's gone up another twenty thousand, Bridge. He means business."

Bridget sat up, suddenly furious. "I mean business, too." She called the bank again and haggled with her representative until he agreed to cover a short-term bridge loan.

Duff got serious. "This is a bad idea, Bee. I mean, I have complete faith in you, but less in Dorset Hills. What if something happens and the pageant doesn't produce like it usually does?"

"It grows every year, and there's no reason to think this one will be any different. I've still got three weeks to drum up new sponsors. I'll make a killing and pay back the bridge loan before the house even closes."

All the humor had gone out of Duff's eyes, and that was rare. "I'd be a terrible friend if I let you do this. Why are you so set on it?"

Bridget stared around again then back at Beau, whose tail continued to fan steadily. "This place just feels right, Duff. I don't want Mr. Slick killing it."

"Ah. So, you're rescuing the house. Just like you rescue dogs."

"I just get a feeling sometimes. It's not as crazy as it sounds."

Rubbing her forehead, Duff sighed. "Okay, fine. We'll top him by five thousand, and not a penny more. I don't care what the bank says. If you have to work more hours waiting tables to carry the mortgage, you'll have less time with the dogs and be miserable."

She submitted the new offer, and then grabbed Bridget's hand. Bridget tried to pull her hand away, preferring to save displays of affection for the dogs. Duffy held onto her fingertips and wouldn't let go.

Bridget leaned back against the headrest and muttered something akin to a prayer.

It was only a couple of minutes till the phone buzzed again. Duff stabbed at it a few times before she could bring up the response. "Oh, Bridget, I'm sorry. He's thrown another fifty grand at them."

She groaned. "Fifty! Oh, man, I hate this guy. Drops that like it's nothing, when it means everything to me."

"It's not personal, Bee. He doesn't know it's you. This is just business."

"Well, that's just as bad. He'll take this place and turn it into something grey and soulless, like the rest of Dorset Hills is becoming. Then he'll flip it and sell to someone else who follows all the City's rules like a robot. They'll get a Labrador retriever, just because it's on the city crest."

Duff released her friend's fingers and typed back a quick response. "I promise I'll find another house that blows you away."

Bridget shook her head. "This is the one."

"There's no 'one' house," Duff argued. "It's not like romance. And even that is a load of crap."

"The premise of my matchmaking is that there is only one perfect match. Call me crazy, but I still believe that—about dogs *and* people."

"Well, it doesn't extend to houses, trust me. I've seen so many people lose their first and even their fifth house and still find what they call 'the one.'"

Bridget turned the key in the ignition. "Call a time of death."

Duff opened the passenger door to climb out just as Mr. Olson came hurrying toward them. Bridget rolled down the window again and he practically stuck his face into the car.

"Bridget, the house is yours," he said. "As long as you can take possession immediately. We need to pack up and move before the twins are born."

"But I can't match the competing offer, Mr. Olson."

"I know, dear. We want you to have it anyway." His face crinkled in a smile.

Bridget hesitated. "That is so kind of you, but you should do what's best for your family."

"That's why we want you to have it—because you helped make our family. Look, the money is already more than we hoped. We're not greedy."

Tears filled Bridget's eyes and spilled down her cheeks. "I can have it?"

"We insist." He jerked his thumb toward the sports car. "That guy wants to knock it down. He's a developer."

"Well, I have to be honest, sir. I'll make some changes, too. I want to turn the barn into a kennel, for starters. But I love the house and I'd never knock it down."

Mr. Olson's eyes filled, too. "Thank you. I know it's just a house but—"

"I'll take good care of it, I promise." Bridget jumped out and hugged him.

Duff was making squawking sounds behind her. Bridget couldn't tell if it was excitement or disapproval. Then she came around the car and hugged both of them. Finally, Mr. Olson pulled away. "My wife will get jealous," he said, laughing.

Duff grabbed Bridget's hands and they jumped up and down. Beau circled them, wanting to get in on the action but too polite to do more than poke at Bridget with his nose. Finally, she knelt and wrapped her arms around him. "Oh, buddy. All of this is ours. The barn, the trails, even a creek apparently. Our luck has finally changed."

Beau licked her left ear. Perhaps that was why she didn't hear the door of the sports car open or the crunch of footfalls on gravel until Sullivan Shaw's Blundstones were planted in front of her, about a foot apart.

"I hate to break up the party," he said. "But may I have a word?"

Still on her knees holding Beau, Bridget looked up. "Sure."

His eyes, a murkier blue than Duff's, widened, and his smile, which had looked fake anyway, vanished completely. "Oh. It's you."

CHAPTER FOUR

Bridget pushed herself up off the gravel and then dusted her knees with both hands. "Yeah. It's me."

Sullivan stuck out his hand cautiously, as if he weren't quite sure what she'd do to it. "Hello again."

"Hey." She gave his hand a quick pump and let go. "Sorry about the house."

"No, you're not." He pushed his hands into the pockets of his black leather jacket. It looked buttery soft. Expensive. Vulnerable to dog incursions.

"Okay, I'm not sorry I got the house," she admitted. "It's a dream come true for me, actually. I don't have the options you have."

He tipped his head quizzically. "You don't know anything about my options. Getting this house was important to me, too. I made a generous offer that was inexplicably declined."

Bridget looked down and scratched Beau's ears. His tail was at half-mast. Guarded. He sensed the guy's anger but didn't realize it was justified. "Look, I got lucky today. I helped the owner's daughter once and he was grateful."

"Bridget." Duff's voice was clipped. "There's no need to explain. The owner made the choice he wanted to make."

"The owner made a choice from his heart instead of his head," Mr. Slick said. "You just cost him and his future grandkids nearly fifty grand. Does that make sense?"

Bridget crossed her arms over her chest. "Not everything has to make sense. I told you that when I—"

He held up his hand. "Turned me down for one of your rescue mutts. I remember."

"That might have hurt your feelings, but it was for the best. It doesn't mean you won't make a good owner to some other dog one day."

His eyes narrowed to blue slits. "Why thank you, Bridget. Your opinion means so much to me."

Duff cleared her throat. "There's no need to—"

Sullivan turned on her. "People like you give real estate agents a bad name."

"Pardon me? How dare you!"

Bridget spoke over her. "Duff, just leave it."

Beau moved into position in front of Bridget and his hackles rose. Sullivan took a step back. "Watch your dog, lady."

"Watch your tone, mister. You sound threatening."

"I'm not threatening anyone. I'm asking you to do the right thing. You're bilking an elderly couple of money they may need later. What if one of their grandkids gets sick?"

Snapping her fingers, Bridget motioned Beau to get behind her. "Look. I was trying to be nice earlier, but here's the truth: the Olsons didn't want the house they loved and raised their kids in bulldozed by a heartless developer."

A flush started at the collar of Sullivan's white T-shirt and raced up his cheeks. "That's—"

"The truth. They were willing to take a loss to leave the

house with someone who cares about it. I plan to live here and treat it like gold."

He started backing away. "Like another pet, you mean."

Bridget shrugged. "I mean I'll love it like you can't, and that mattered to the Olsons more than your offer."

Shaking his head, he stopped. "You don't know what you're getting yourself into, Bridget. That inspection they commissioned missed a few things. Unless rescuing dogs brings in bigger bucks than I think it does, you're going to struggle here."

"Sour grapes," Duff said. "The inspection was done by the biggest firm in Dorset Hills."

"Commissioned by the seller, not the buyer," Sullivan said. "It's an important distinction."

"I'm aware of that," Duff snapped back. "This is going to work out fine, and I'd appreciate it if you didn't scare my client."

"I'm trying to *spare* your client. This house could turn into an epic money pit. Bridget, there are other properties that are better value in your price range."

"Then why are you wasting your time here? Go buy them."

He sighed. "You don't deserve this, but I'm going to make you an offer you shouldn't refuse: I'll pay you fifty thousand if you'll step back from this deal and let the owners take the offer I made. They're ahead, you're ahead."

"And you're where? Behind?"

"In the short term, yes, I certainly am. But down the road, we'll all be further ahead."

"No thank you," Bridget said. "I want this house."

"You're being unreasonable."

"Thinking with my heart? Guilty as charged."

Turning to Duff, he said, "Can't you talk some sense into her? I can tell you know I'm right."

Duff caught Bridget's sleeve. "Maybe we should take a minute to discuss this."

"I don't need a minute." Bridget had always been slow to work up to a change, but once a decision was made, there was no going back. "The house is mine. Let the chips fall where they may."

Sullivan threw up his hands and turned to walk away. "That's not all that's going to fall, lady. Shingles will be raining down on you in no time." Slowing, he turned back. "But I guess you're hard-headed."

"I've been called worse."

"I have no doubt of that."

She raised a warning hand. "Wait!"

He dismissed her with a wave and turned just a second too late to see the large, deep puddle in his path. The water sloshed over his Blundstones and he just stood there for a moment. Then he proceeded on to his car. Kicking off the boots, he tossed them on the floor in the back seat, before folding himself behind the wheel again.

Bridget and Duff tried to hold it together until he drove off but failed spectacularly. They were laughing so hard that Beau got worried and started prancing erratically between them.

"It's okay, Beau, it's okay. We're going to be so happy here." She raised crossed fingers at Duff. "As long as the bank doesn't foreclose on us."

CHAPTER FIVE

B one Appetit Bistro was little more than a diner with big ambitions. It was situated directly across a small square from St. Elgin Manor, Dorset Hills' only museum. Business had always been decent, but it picked up even more after the museum's recent installation of a pair of bronze cane corsi, or Italian mastiffs, on either side of the manor's double front doors. The fearsome-looking dogs rather dwarfed the estate, which had long ago belonged to one of the town's founding families, but they were among the most popular in the city's new bronze collection. The bus tour stopped at the museum for at least an hour and most people never bothered to go inside. After posing with the corsi, they came over to Boners, as the diner was commonly called.

Like many of Dorset Hills' restaurants, shops and services, Bone Appetit fully exploited the canine angle. The walls were covered in kitschy dog portraits on black velvet. The paper place mats featured thirty different breeds that could be colored with the rainbow of pencil crayons sitting in a milkshake glass on every table. Even the menu was sprinkled with dog-themed illustrations highlighting such crowd pleasers as the Doggone Best Burger, and the Kibbles and Bits Brownie Sundae. The serving staff wore aprons adorned with a knockoff of Snoopy dancing. It was the type of thing that usually made Bridget cringe, but as she tied the straps behind her on the morning after buying her house, she was inclined to do the Snoopy dance, too.

Grabbing the coffee pot, she started circulating. Boners' bottomless cup was a huge draw, especially with the regulars.

"How's it going, Trent?" she asked, topping up his mug.

"It's a good day," he said. "I'm on the right side of the grass."

Bridget smiled, as if it were the first time she'd heard the joke. Trent Fenton was the most regular of the regulars. A retired cop, he needed somewhere to go every morning, and he always sat in Bridget's section.

She buzzed around her tables, dropping greetings and nectar into coffee cups. There was a mail carrier on break, a crossing guard before the school rush, and a couple of fire-fighters coming off their shift. Some of the guys flirted with Bridget, and she patted their shoulders absentmindedly, like so many dogs.

When she reached the lone woman in the restaurant, she stopped. "More hot water, Grace?"

Grace Greenwood could work a teabag like it was nobody's business. After several refills, the water in her cup was barely tan. She was more quirky than cheap. For starters, she always used powdered sweetener she brought in a pill bottle rather than the packets on the table. She also carried her own dried fruit and nuts, which she added to the breakfast yogurt parfait, or later, to the Bone Appetit house salad. Bridget did her best to indulge her customers' idiosyncrasies, in the hopes that tips would follow. Grace was surprisingly generous for someone who wouldn't spring for a fresh teabag.

Without waiting for Grace's nod, Bridget picked up the small stainless steel teapot and headed back to the counter. On the way, she collected Gerry Brecht's half-eaten omelet. One of the town's two computer whizzes, he was in the habit of sending back most of his meals midway through, declaring them inedible. The second order always went down smoothly. It was an annoying ploy that wasted perfectly good food, but Frank Mason, the owner, couldn't be bothered making a fuss about it. Bridget didn't either, even though Gerry had only once left a tip, and then probably by accident.

"You're smiling," Frank said, coming out of the kitchen. "What's wrong?"

Frank's deadpan delivery had improved over the many years Bridget had known him. Now closing in on 70, his well-lined face, bushy eyebrows and shiny bald head were the perfect canvas for comedy.

Rachel, the other full-time waitress, reacted as usual by smacking him with whatever was at hand—in this case a spoon. It was only seven thirty a.m., but she had a full face of makeup under backcombed silvery hair. "Oh, Frank, you're terrible."

"What? I'm serious," he persisted. "I can count on two hands the number of times I've seen Bridget smile. Usually it's when she's pranked me, or I've sat on ketchup or something."

Bridget laughed. "Come on, Frank. I'm not that bad."

"Now she's laughing." Frank looked up at the ceiling. "Is there a pail of water rigged up to drown me?"

"Just stop, Frank," Rachel said. "You'll make her self-conscious and she'll never laugh again. I, for one, like the sound of it."

"I dunno. Something's up." Frank buttoned his striped uniform shirt up to his neck and shivered. "Scary."

Rachel set a mug on the counter, filled it with coffee from a fresh pot and slid it across the counter toward Bridget. "Just ignore Frank. But you did arrive early, hon, and that sets off some warning bells, even for me."

Bridget drained half of her coffee at a gulp and fanned her mouth. Then she delivered Grace's hot water, along with Gerry's second, somewhat smaller, omelet. Frank had cut it down by one egg in a quiet protest. If Gerry noticed the shrinkage, he said nothing. As usual, he was coloring the dogs on his place mat. Every visit, he filled in the same six terriers with the pencil crayons on hand. The results were often quite pretty, if unrealistic.

"Two protein shakes for the firefighters," she told Frank. "Three raw eggs apiece."

He shook his head. "No raw eggs in my restaurant. I'm not getting closed down for salmonella."

Bridget addressed the impasse by delivering the drinks in tall glasses and setting a carton of eggs, a bowl and a whisk on the firefighters' table. "At your own risk, gentlemen."

When her section had settled, Bridget perched in front of the counter on a chrome stool covered in red vinyl. "I have news," she said, kicking off and spinning around. "I bought a house."

Squealing, Rachel ran around the counter, slowed Bridget's spin and hugged her. "That's wonderful, hon. Where?"

"Pemsville?" Frank asked, sounding hopeful.

Bridget scowled at him. "No such luck, Frank. I'm not quitting and moving to another town."

"I didn't mean that." He fought a smirk, as he started to roll cutlery in paper serviettes.

"Yeah, you did. But I'm not taking it personally."

The smirk bloomed fully. "Take it personally. It is personal."

"Aw, Frank, don't kill my buzz. Not when I'm going to ask you for a raise."

Frank stopped wrapping cutlery and stood perfectly still.

Rachel laughed. "You can freeze but we still see you, Frank."

He licked his lips, as if the bistro had gone suddenly dry. "Tell me she's joking."

"She's joking," Rachel said. "We're just not used to it."

"Not joking, actually," Bridget said. "I need a raise, Frank. The house was more than I bargained for, and moving costs are coming up sooner than I could have imagined."

"Your problem is now my problem?" he said.

"We're practically family, right? You treat me like a kid most of the time."

Frank's hand twitched toward the pile of cutlery but didn't connect. "There's a reason I didn't reproduce. Kids drain you dry."

"Your 'work wife' could use a raise, too. Right, Rachel?"

"I'd faint first and then cry." Rachel's laugh filled the restaurant.

Covering his ears, Frank chanted, "Can't hear you, can't hear you."

Bridget tugged at his sleeve. "Come on, Frank, puleeze. I've never had a raise in five years of working here."

The cutlery clattered as he went back to wrapping it. "A raise usually reflects exceeding expectations, right? And I gotta say, you don't always. Some customers are scared to sit in your section. Like I mentioned, you've only smiled seven times in five years. Not that anyone's counting."

"You're exaggerating." Bridget threw in another smile for good measure. It felt foreign, as if her facial muscles had gotten rusty. "Smile or no smile, my section is usually full all day."

"With your buddies, yeah."

"My buddies and my clients, and the sponsors for that huge event I throw every year. They all sit in my section, and they buy lots of Doggone Burgers."

"Most of your friends are vegans who pressure me to add legumes to the menu."

"Frank, I may not be as sweet as Rachel—"

"You're lovely, hon," Rachel said. "An acquired taste."

Frank gave up and let the cutlery drop. "I'm sure you're yanking my chain like usual."

Bridget pushed off and spun around again. "Not yanking your chain, boss. I really would like a raise, please. And if you do, I promise to bring in even more big sponsors and convert them to the Boners magic."

He shuddered. "Don't call it that."

"Everyone calls it that. At least everyone with a sense of humor. And they're the only people who matter."

"Like you would know," he muttered.

"Oh, Frank, I laugh. I laugh all the time. I just do it on the inside, so no one sees." She stopped spinning and grinned at him. "Isn't it better that way?"

He flicked a nervous glance at her grin. "Yeah. Put those fangs away."

"And if I do?"

"Stop scaring people and you'll get your raise. Your tips might go up, too."

"I'll keep scaring people, bring more sponsors in, and you'll give me and Rachel a raise. Deal?"

"I'm missing what's in it for me, exactly," he said. "You'd bring these people in anyway because it's easier to meet during your shift."

"He's got you there, Bee," Rachel said, topping up Bridget's coffee.

"True," Bridget said. "So you've left me no choice but to point this out, Frank: You like me." She held up her hand. "Yes, I also annoy you. But the fact that I've had a key to Boners for four years and you trust me with the bookwork and your bank accounts suggests you also want me around. You just like complaining about me so that you don't have to pay me more."

"You've got him there, Bee," Rachel said. "You could give yourself a raise and he wouldn't notice."

"Correct. Because he can't remember his own passwords."

Frank sighed. "I need you, but I could do without your attitude."

Bridget leaned across the counter and kissed his cheek. "My attitude is part of my charm. It keeps the customers coming back for more."

"Don't push it, Bee."

She knew their banter was mostly in fun, but still it bothered her a little. Why wasn't it enough to offer good service without being phoney? "With all I have on the go, I still never miss a shift, Frank."

"You're reliable, both of you," Frank said, relenting. "Bone Appetit wouldn't be the same without you. For better or worse."

"So, I can give us a raise next time I do payroll?"

"You win." He started in on the cutlery again. "Just try not to scare new customers, okay? Hallowe'en's over and Dorset Hills is moving into the season of giving thanks."

Bridget raised her coffee cup. "I give thanks to you, Frank. And I'm going to show my gratitude by not pulling a single prank on you this month."

He pointed at her with a knife. "If you can make it to Christmas, I'll up you another fifty cents an hour."

Bridget joined him in rolling the cutlery. "Excellent. I guess I'm not above a little fakery when it comes to paying my mortgage."

Frank left the cutlery, sat down on the stool she'd vacated, and spun. "Sounds like we're in for quite a ride."

CHAPTER SIX

Bridget wandered from room to room, a sloppy smile on her face. It was hard to believe that less than a week after she laid eyes on it, the house was already hers. The Olsons' daughter had delivered early, so they hired a company to pack and move them in short order. Bridget had her own small army to do the same.

"Aw, look, Bridget's in love," said Cori Hogan. She was pulling pots and pans out of a cardboard box and then stacking them in the kitchen cupboard. "Did anyone ever think they'd live to see it?"

"I did." Duff pushed up the sleeves of her cashmere sweater. Yanking on yellow rubber gloves, she opened the fridge door. "I just hoped it would be with a human."

"You don't need to clean the fridge, Duff." Bridget circled open boxes with Beau at her side. "The Olsons left the place in good shape."

In her sky-high heels and designer jeans, Duff had been working harder than anyone, but she had good help. The five women, known among themselves as the "Rescue

Mafia," had sprung into action when the movers left. In just a few hours, they'd nearly finished unpacking and setting up. Bridget had never been one to accumulate stuff, so it wasn't a huge job.

As the women moved quickly, dogs of every shape and color wove among them, investigating their new home. Somehow, no one tripped. It was like the action had been carefully choreographed.

Maisie Todd, a dog groomer, was on a stepladder trying to change a lightbulb. "This thing is stuck."

"Let me try," Duff said, pulling off her rubber gloves.

"Be my guest." Maisie backed down the ladder. She had crazy corkscrew golden curls and a cherubic face, but her rosebud mouth was no stranger to F-bombs.

Bridget watched as Duff quickly scaled the ladder. "Wow, you really can leap tall buildings in heels."

Pushing glossy hair behind her ears, Duff grinned down at her. "Absolutely. But I've never been good with home repairs, I'm afraid. That's what men are for."

"Oh, please," Cori said. "We don't need a guy for this. We're capable women."

She went up the ladder next, climbing to the very top. Small and fine-boned, with short dark hair and brown eyes, Cori had the most commanding presence of all of them. Dogs that outweighed her obeyed without question, and that gift made her the most popular trainer in town.

"This is stupid." Cori leapt off the ladder and landed lightly. "We moved a five-ton dresser to the basement and we can't do this?"

"How many dog rescuers does it take to change a lightbulb?" asked Nika Lothian, getting ready to take her shot. She was the sweetest of the group, and arguably the prettiest, with her smooth brown skin, black hair and striking amber eyes that glowed with warmth. As a veterinary technician, she was invaluable in keeping all their pets healthy.

As Nika came back down the ladder, Maisie laughed. "We can turn a feral wolf-cross into a lapdog together, but we can't change a lightbulb."

"My turn," Bridget said. "If anyone's going to break it, it should be me." Sure enough, with one twist, the glass bulb came away in her hand, leaving the metal base stuck in the socket. "Well, that sucks."

"I've got a guy," Duff said.

"You've got a guy?" Maisie and Nika spoke over each other.

"She's always got a guy," Bridget said. "The bigger question is... what's happened to the rest of the harem?"

Duff shook a rubber-gloved finger as she went back to the fridge. "I meant I have a handyman who can help with repairs around here."

"I want a handyman," Nika said, dreamily. "Is he single?"

"He is." Duff laughed ruefully. "I just cut him loose and I'd be pleased to see him well-homed with one of you."

"Let's let Bridget work her magic," Maisie said, filling the upper cupboards with dishes. "She's the professional matchmaker."

Bridget snorted from the top of the ladder, where she was trying to pry the metal from the light socket with her fingernails. "It's accidental. I'd never call myself a pro."

"Yet more than twenty couples credit their relationships to you," Duff said. "Not to mention the others that won't admit it."

"I match dogs with people," Bridget said. "The human hookups are collateral damage."

Bridget was happy to brag about her record with dogs,

but the other matches somewhat baffled her. It was true that pageant participants often paired up, but it seemed mostly the result of bringing dog lovers together.

"That only adds to your mystique," Duff said, her voice muffled by the fridge.

"How is it that the matchmaker's friends are all single?" Maisie asked, starting to line up canned goods on a shelf.

"It's a 'shoemaker's wife goes barefoot' situation," Nika said. "Get on it, Bee. We're all amazing."

"That you are." Bridget smiled down at four faces, each a unique flower in a bouquet of friends. "More than you know."

"Then why?" Maisie pressed.

Bridget didn't have a good answer, or at least one she cared to share. She suspected they were an acquired taste, just as she was. They were all attractive, talented and kind-hearted. But like most people who'd seen many animals suffering and abandoned, they could be cynical and guarded.

"I'll tell you why," Cori said, smirking. "We're bitches."

There was a squawk of indignation, and Bridget's laughter floated over the hubbub.

"Speak for yourself," Nika said.

"I am. I'm a bitch and proud of it."

"Well, I'm not," Nika said.

Cori dropped one pot into another to make a statement. "Self-awareness, Nika. I've seen you hiss like a rabid racoon at abusive dog owners."

"I do not!"

"You do, Nika. We all do. I'm not saying it's a bad thing. But it's true. Ask Duffer."

Duff was more like an honorary member of the Rescue

Mafia. Her work as a real estate agent meant she needed to keep her nose pretty clean. She tended to help out behind the scenes, and at the pageant.

Rescuing dogs could be a touchy topic in Dorset Hills. In a city known for its dog-friendly ways, that some should be neglected, cast off or worse was hard to admit for civic leaders. City Council backed the annual rescue pageant but allocated minimal funding for animal services. When legit channels failed pets in need, the Rescue Mafia sometimes worked like thieves in the night. As part of a wider network that spanned other Hills communities, they had war stories galore.

But today they could put down their swords. It was a celebration.

"Don't put me on the spot, Cori," Duff said. "You're all wonderful, and I'm not the matchmaker, anyway."

"But you're the only one of us who dates regularly," Nika said. "What's your secret? I mean, aside from the heels."

Duff laughed. "If there's a secret, it *is* the heels. Or more specifically, in acting feminine." Objections began and she raised her hand. "You asked! I may not be as capable of scaling a fence and liberating a neglected dog as you are, but when it comes to dating, I know a few things. Basically, I try to put on the girl."

"So, be fake, you mean?" Cori said.

"See, this is why I didn't want to be dragged into the discussion." Duff loaded produce into a fridge drawer with too much force. "I'm not faking anything. It's all me."

"What do you think, Bee?" Maisie asked. "Are we scaring men away?"

"If they're so easily scared they're not worth having,"

Bridget said. "Besides, if there's one thing I've learned in rescue, there's a lid for every pot. Your numbers will come up eventually, and if I have any magic touch at all, you can be sure I'll help."

Mollified, Maisie offered Bridget a set of pliers. "Give those a try."

"Uh-uh. Leave the light alone, Bee," Duff said. "Getting electrocuted before the pageant is a bad idea."

"Afterwards wouldn't be ideal either," Bridget said. "I have one helluva mortgage to pay."

"It'll work out fine." Duff buffed the fridge door with a dish towel. "Now to decorate the place."

"It's already perfect," Bridget said, glancing over the kitchen and living room. "But you can do what you like, as long as it's not dog-kitschy. I get enough of that at work."

"Nearly done, and it's not even four o'clock," Nika said. "How about I make my famous chili for dinner?"

Bridget noticed that Beau was pacing back and forth by the low front windows of the living room. "What's wrong, buddy?"

Cori looked around quickly. "Head count!"

She called out the dogs' names one by one and they came and sat in front of her. Where there should have been 13, there were 12.

"Fritz!" they all yelled at once. The gray-and-white terrier mix did not appear.

"Spread out and search," Cori said, assigning each of them an area of the house. They deployed without question. When it came to this sort of thing, the trainer ruled humans as well as dogs.

Five minutes later, they regrouped. No Fritz. "Could he have gotten out with the movers?" Bridget fretted. "He'll have no idea where he is. What if he tries to get back to my old place?"

"Relax," Cori said. "He won't have gone far, and it's a nice day. Let's get moving before we lose the light. We'll fan out and find him in no time."

They grabbed their coats and gathered at the door. The housewarming effervescence had evaporated.

Maisie went out first. She stopped suddenly and they smacked into her from behind.

Slipping around them to see what had caused the jam, Bridget came face to face with Sullivan Shaw. He was standing in the middle of the parking area. Under the arm of his leather jacket was Fritz.

"What are you doing here?" Bridget asked. "And how did you get my dog?"

Fritz struggled to get down but Shaw held onto him. "This little charmer knocked over my trash can and spread the remains of my week all over the driveway. I figured he belonged here and came over to ask."

"Your trash can?" Bridget asked. "Where exactly is that?"

"Right outside my house," he said, smirking. "Which happens to be on the other side of your barn. I guess you didn't bother checking out the neighbors before making an offer. Let alone checking out the house itself."

A fire started in the pit of Bridget's stomach. If she'd had something to throw at that smirk without risk of hitting the dog, she might have.

Duff moved through the women and blocked Bridget. "Thanks for bringing Fritz back, Sullivan. It's nice to have good neighbors."

Sullivan set Fritz on the ground and the dog trotted over

to Cori and sat down in front of her. "Good boy," she said. "You little brat."

The other dogs pushed between knees and feet, and then surged down the stairs to greet Sullivan with enthusiasm. Only Beau held back. His tail dropped gradually, as if he didn't want to be blatantly rude. He didn't like Sullivan, and he certainly wasn't a faker.

"Do you mind?" Sullivan said, as muzzles poked and prodded him according to the dog's height. Fritz pawed at his Blundstones, which had apparently survived the puddle. Morty the Lab mix and Lulu the collie got a lot more personal. Shaw raised his knee and pushed the dogs gently away.

"They smell something good," Cori said.

Sullivan raised his eyebrows and Cori's face reddened. Bridget didn't remember seeing her warrior friend blush before.

"Are you packing liver treats?" Cori asked.

"Why would I carry liver treats? I don't have a dog."

"Oh. I'm sorry." Cori's tone made it clear that a man without a dog was a pitiful thing indeed.

"I'm not. This crew seems like trouble." He threw Bridget a glare. "I'd ask you to keep them on your property —since you didn't want it to be *my* property. We don't all have fences out here."

"So, *this* is the guy." Cori turned to Bridget. "The sore loser who tried to bribe you."

"Cori, please," Bridget said. "We're neighbors now, apparently. And Fritz was just picking through his garbage."

Cori picked Fritz up and held him in front of her face. He tried to lick her nose. "Good thing we have a few weeks before the pageant, pal, because you're not perfect yet."

Sullivan snorted. "He tried to nip me on the way over."

"He was just scared," Cori said. "If a strange man picked you up, you'd nip, too."

"I'd do worse than that," Sullivan said.

The women laughed, including Cori. Sullivan grudgingly smiled, too.

Seeing a chink in his armor, Duff stepped forward. "Could I ask you a favor, Sullivan? We've got a little problem none of us can solve."

"I've got to get home," Sullivan said.

"It'll only take a minute, honestly." Duff's voice was like honey, golden and sweet. "If you don't mind."

"Well, okay." He came toward the house and the women scattered. Cori, Maisie and Nika went down the stairs, and Bridget and Duff backed inside.

In the kitchen, Duff handed him the pliers and gestured toward the ladder. "Each one of us has tried to get what's left of a lightbulb out of that socket. And failed, I'm afraid. I think we need a man's touch."

Shaking his head, Sullivan said, "Are you trying to manipulate me or electrocute me?"

"Neither," she said. "I'm trying to ease neighborly relations for my friend. Is it working?"

"Turn off the switch and I'll see what I can do." He climbed the ladder and took care of the problem in about fifteen seconds. Climbing back down, he handed the pliers to Bridget instead of Duff. "That's just the beginning of stuff that's going to fall apart here."

Bridget opened her mouth but Duff spoke before she could. "We'll hire the help we need. But thanks to you, we have enough light to cook dinner."

"And count the mutts, I hope," he said.

"Would you like to stay for a bite?" Duff asked. "Nika makes a mean vegan chilli."

He was backing toward the door. "I'm good. You ladies enjoy your housewarming," he said. They all followed him out and somehow, he nearly stepped into the exact same puddle as he had a few days earlier.

"Careful," Bridget called, and he dodged at the last minute, with surprising grace.

"Fill that in, will you?" he said. "It's a drowning hazard."

She thought he laughed as he disappeared into the bushes but she wasn't quite sure.

"Oh my gosh," Maisie said, once they were back inside. "That guy is so hot."

"He's an ass," Bridget said.

"Full of himself," Cori said.

"He seemed nice to me." Nika pulled tinned beans off the shelf and then dug around in the drawer for the can opener. "Very nice."

"He's all those things," Duff said. "A mutt, like everyone else. He's just upset about losing the house. Still, he did the right thing with Fritz."

"I saw how you worked your wiles on him, Duff," Nika said. "I gotta try that."

Duff smiled. "I wouldn't waste your efforts on Sullivan. He's only got eyes for Bridget, I'm afraid."

"What?" Bridget turned from the cupboard, bowls in hand. "He was glaring at me."

"He only took his eyes off you to fix the light. Just an observation."

The bowls clattered as Bridget set them down hard. "He must be calculating what it would take to poison me, or something."

"Or marry you and claim the house for his own," Nika said. "There's more than one way to get the deed for a place."

"I'll take the poisoning, thanks." Bridget went over to the couch and wedged herself in between three dogs. "Sullivan Shaw may be hot, but we'd be a match made in hell."

CHAPTER SEVEN

Bridget smelled a rat. Or possibly a hamster, a gerbil, or even a guinea pig. Her sense of smell wasn't refined enough to distinguish one rodent over another, but she knew exactly where it had lived last, because Beau had gone into a point. Aiming his long muzzle toward a corner, he lifted his right front paw and then froze. Bridget had never trained him to point but there were sporting dogs in his background. She knew that because she'd submitted his DNA for testing, as she did all of her rescues. Subtle differences in breed traits could help in handling and motivating a dog to learn. More knowledge never hurt, she figured.

Today, Beau's Irish setter genes pointed to a possible lie in Ross Stanley's application for one of Bridget's rescues. Her 20-page questionnaire—part one of the application process—specifically asked if there were small animals in the home. Bridget had nothing against rodents, but her goal was to set her dogs up for success, and depending on the dog's proclivities, a hamster could be a tasty temptation. That would be bad for her reputation and worse for the hamster.

Crossing Ross' living room, she made a show of glancing out the window before inspecting the floor in the corner. Sure enough, there were stray curls of wood shavings, and a couple of sunflower seeds by her feet.

She turned back to Ross. "Nice view of the park."

"It's the highest rated dog park in Dorset Hills," Ross said. "As you probably know."

He gestured to the couch and Bridget perched on the edge. Meanwhile, Beau did a circuit of the room, nose to the ground, reading all there was to be read.

"Any small pets?" she asked. "Hamsters, rats, gerbils or the like?"

"Nope, not a fan," Ross said, smiling.

Strike one. A brazen lie, offered with a smile. She jotted some words in a spiral-bound notepad, none of them flattering. "How about children?"

"Nope, no kids."

"Nieces and nephews? Occasional young visitors?"

"No. Why?" Ross shifted uneasily, as if suddenly aware of the Cheerios and Goldfish crackers under his chair. Further back was a small doll with pink hair.

Strike two. Another lie. There had certainly been a child around, and it was only a matter of time before Beau vacuumed up some of the evidence.

Bridget had nothing against children, either. Her dogs were well socialized with kids, but there was no telling how good the children were with dogs. As much as she loved her furry charges, Bridget was under no delusions. They were animals, plain and simple. All the training in the world couldn't guarantee a rescue dog with a troubled past would tolerate a child pulling its tail and ears or riding it like a stallion. Kids might come into the picture later, but by then everyone would have a chance to adjust. It was her job to reduce risk upfront, even if that meant discriminating against families and rodents. There was never a shortage of people competing for her dogs, so she could afford to be choosy.

"I just like to confirm the information in your application," she said. "Sometimes circumstances change in the months after people submit."

"Nothing's changed. Still just your average single guy wanting a dog buddy."

"Well, you have a lovely home." Bridget got up. "Do you mind if I use the washroom?"

While the water ran in the sink, she took a peek underneath. Shampoo and conditioner for color-treated, curly hair. Both bottles damp and recently used.

Strike three. Ross was nearly bald and had little use for premium hair products. Someone else must have stopped by for a shower.

If Bridget had to guess, Ross was probably dating a woman with frizzy hair whose little girl owned a hamster. Maybe it was too early in their relationship to make it official on his application. She understood that, but the fact remained that he had misrepresented the truth. If he lied about the basics, then what else?

It was always disappointing to discover people weren't forthright, but in the end, it didn't matter that much. Even if everything he'd said had checked out perfectly, Ross would never have been a pageant contender simply because he'd failed the sniff test. Beau's, not Bridget's. The dog had given Ross' hand a cursory inspection when they arrived, and then turned away slightly. More telling was Beau's tail. Its gentle wave slowed, then stopped, and finally dropped. Once that tail sank, you were toast. She had never known Beau to change his mind about anyone.

Sometimes the reasons for Beau's strong opinion surfaced quickly. Other times, she just had to take his word for it. She trusted him implicitly.

Bridget couldn't tell Ross he'd been failed by a dog, of course. In fact, she didn't tell anyone how she really made her decisions. Every year the pageant brought in thousands of charitable dollars from sponsors, organizations and regular contributors. They liked to think there was rigor behind her method. And there was. Her seven-step screening process consisted of a written application, a phone interview, a personal video of the applicant's home and neighborhood, an in-person interview, a series of lectures, a hands-on training test, and a team-building community activity on the day of the actual pageant.

Even before Beau arrived, Bridget's success rate was impressive. In fact, she'd never had a dog returned. Not once, with more than a hundred dogs placed. Her screening worked well, but it wasn't easy. Many people passed the test with flying colors, so the final choice came down to intangibles. Bridget trusted her own intuition, but she trusted Beau's even more. Unlike her, he never had a moment of self-doubt. He wasn't swayed by emotional cases, and he felt no guilt over turning down perfectly decent people. No matter what decision his tail conveyed, he slept well at night. The same couldn't be said for Bridget.

Now she had to go through the motions of being polite to Ross when he was doomed to be dogless, at least through this channel. She couldn't leave right away. It had to look like a fair, considered process. And she had to leave him with hope, because the finalists wouldn't be announced for another week. Bridget hated giving false hope to people who didn't stand a chance, but what was a contest without suspense and surprise?

Her phone buzzed and relief flooded through her. She'd initially resisted Duff's suggestion of tag-teaming for these visits, but even with Beau at her side, she'd always felt vulnerable in strangers' homes. She'd seen odd things over the years, and some potentially dangerous things. Having backup was safer, and she billed it as quality control. Now there were two sets of eyes and ears, not counting Beau's.

Duff blew into the apartment like a breath of fresh air. Her cheeks were pink from the brisk day, but there wasn't a hair out of place. She quizzed Ross lightly and quickly, and then whisked Bridget out the door.

"That guy had fail written all over him," she said, once they were safely in Bridget's car.

"Right? Do you think he knew?" Bridget pulled out of the parking lot and headed into the city core.

Duff shook her head. "You have a great poker face. I barely know when you're telling the truth. Only your mom could tell."

"Bet I could fool her, too." Bridget smiled, but it didn't linger. Of all the places they'd lived, her mom had most hated their two-year stint in Dorset Hills. The town was "too full of itself," she'd said. Bridget didn't disagree. Yet when she finished college, she'd fallen for Dorset Hills' siren call. All she knew then was that she wanted a life filled with dogs, and this town could give that to her. Now, she had exactly what she wanted, but a pack of dogs made travelling difficult. Her mom had visited once after Bridget's dad passed, but it felt like she couldn't get out of Dog Town fast enough. Sometimes Bridget felt adrift in the world, but she had Beau, of course, and the Rescue Mafia became more of an anchor every year.

"Left on Main, right on Deerbourne," Duff said, pulling out her phone. "Let's keep Trixie on track so that we can grab a coffee before the last home visit. Remind me why you cram so many into November?"

"Because whatever people tell me in spring is out of date by November. I need to know exactly what I'm dealing with right before the pageant."

"So it ends up being your worst month... and your best month?"

"Pretty much. Then layer on the new house stuff this year. I don't know what I'd do without my Mafia."

"You know we'd do anything for you," Duff said, as Bridget parked outside the next applicant's apartment building.

Trixie Dayton greeted them in the lobby, and there was almost no need to go upstairs to her fifth-floor apartment. Beau liked her. He really liked her. The typically reserved dog practically danced around her.

"Beau, settle," Bridget said. "Did you roll in dognip, Trixie?"

Trixie laughed, brown eyes nearly disappearing into round cheeks. It seemed like she must be as sweet and decent as she smelled to Beau. Nonetheless, she apologized on the elevator about the size of her apartment, its location, and her average-paying office job. "But I promise you, if I got one of your dogs, I'd treat it like a queen. Or a king."

Bridget was expecting a shoebox, but the apartment was a decent size. A dog could practically live in a closet as long as its owner was prepared to get out and have fun with it. At least, her rescue dogs could.

As Trixie showed them around, Beau's tail fanned steadily. Normally he'd have settled into calm nonchalance by now. Trixie was in his top five—a definite contender for the pageant.

"No other pets?" Bridget asked, as she sat down next to Duff, and across from Trixie.

Trixie shook her head. "My last dog died a year ago and I haven't been ready."

"I'm sorry," Bridget said. "What happened?"

"King was twelve, and his kidneys failed." Her eyes filled and spilled over. "I would have done anything, but the vet said he was suffering."

Beau moved close enough to invite a pat on the shoulder. He never offered his head to someone he didn't know well; even then it was a privilege he preferred to reserve for Bridget.

Trixie paused with hand raised and looked to Bridget. Before she could nod approval, Beau had shoved himself under her hand. They all laughed. Running her hands over Beau's shoulder and back, Trixie calmed immediately. They went on with the interview, and Duff typed notes into her phone.

"Are you sure you're ready for a new dog?" Bridget asked.

Pressing her palms into her eyes, Trixie shook her head. "I always said King was the dog of my heart. Do you think it's possible to have two like that in one lifetime?"

Bridget looked at Beau, the dog of her heart, knowing there was no way another dog could replace him. Not in this lifetime, or even the next if there was one.

"Here's what I think," she began. "You're not even thirty, Trixie. You got lucky early. But you can't go the rest of your life with only the memory of one great dog. Each one will be different, and they may not all be superstars, but I guarantee you'll love them."

"Yours are all superstars," Duff said.

"True that," Bridget said, and they laughed.

Trixie turned to Duff. "Do you have one of Bridget's rescues?"

Duff jumped to her feet. "We're done here, right?"

"Trixie, Duff had the perfect dog once, too," Bridget said. "She was only 12 when she lost him, and she won't try again. Isn't that tragic?"

"I'm so sorry," Trixie said. "You should try again, Duff."

"Some day," Duff said. "Maybe. Anyway, we've got to run. See you on Thanksgiving."

"Come ready to win, Trixie," Bridget said, as they walked out. "Don't be Duff."

Duff cuffed her friend as they walked back to the elevator. "Must you? Some of us are satisfied living dog-free."

"I must." Darting ahead, Bridget and Beau played a little game of chase on the way to the parking lot. "Because I know how much you'd love a dog. I will hook you up yet, Duffers."

"Save your matchmaking for people who need it," Duff said. "I bet you get Trixie a dog *and* a boyfriend."

Opening the passenger door with a flourish, Bridget said, "Let's see what magic this pageant brings."

Duff waited till they were on the road before pulling a sheaf of papers out of her purse. "Let's see what money this pageant brings."

"Must *you?* Must you drag my vocation down to that level?"

"I must. Because I know what's riding on this event." She waved a spreadsheet under Bridget's nose. "I've got a few ideas to streamline operations."

Bridget's eyebrows shot up. "A few? That looks like a complete overhaul of my life."

"Oh, relax. I just want this year's pageant to be the best ever."

Making the next turn with one hand, Bridget patted her friend's arm. "You relax. I know you're worried I've overextended myself with the house."

"You did overextend yourself with the house. And I let it happen. Therefore, I'm invested in your success."

Finding a parking spot near Bellington Square was difficult but Bridget eased the van into a tight spot. "My system works just fine, and every year the pageant does better. You said so yourself."

Leaving Beau behind, they walked to Puccini Café, where the coffee was great and the people-watching fantastic. They took a seat by the window and Duff signaled a waitress.

"That's true," Duff said. "But once I started thinking about it, I could see that you were ready to take this to the next level."

Bridget glanced at the spreadsheet. "What's the next level?"

Tapping the spreadsheet with a maroon fingernail, Duff said, "Sponsors. More sponsors. Better sponsors. Every year, you get the same old mom and pop businesses to back the pageant. Yet this is one of the biggest draws on the Dog Town calendar."

"When I tried getting bigger sponsors everyone turned me down."

"That was then, this is now. Look around, Bee. Things are changing in Dog Town."

Duff gestured across the street. On the sidewalk in front of another café called Barkingham Palace sat a statue of a corgi.

"What the hell?" Bridget said. "I thought only public institutions could have the bronzes."

"Look closer."

Bridget practically pressed her nose to the glass. "The proportions are wrong. Its muzzle is snubbed. Wait... is that a knockoff?"

"Yep. I knocked on it yesterday. Fiberglass."

"Oh my." Bridget tried to keep a straight face as the waitress set a large latte in front of each of them. "What's City Council going to do?"

"I give that corgi a few weeks, tops. And there's a weird-looking spaniel over on Mortimer that's not regulation, either."

Taking a sip, Bridget tried to make sense of it all. "What's going on? What are you hearing?"

Leaning closer, Duff whispered, "Not everyone's impressed with Bill Bradshaw."

The new mayor had taken office in June, right before the summer slowdown. He'd made only a few public appearances, including riding a float in the Labor Day Parade. There had been photos in the *Dorset Hills Expositor* of Mayor Bradshaw in a tux at a gallery opening. He was tall, handsome and permanently tanned, like some movie star her mom had always liked.

"He's not folksy like Stan Thompson," Bridget said. "Always liked him. Shame he got voted out."

Duff shook a bit of sugar over her latte. "Bill Bradshaw comes from old money and big business. I've heard he cares about appearances. A lot."

"So, the corgi... that's like flipping the bird to Mayor Bradshaw?"

"Testing the waters, I'm guessing."

Bridget tried to catch up with Duff's thinking. "Are you saying I need to care more about appearances?"

Duff met her eyes as she stirred her coffee. "I think it would help grab the mayor's attention."

"But I don't—"

"—care about appearances. I know, Bee, and I love that about you. But sometimes you need to play the game to get ahead."

"I'm not playing any games."

Taking a long sip, Duff rolled her eyes. "The pageant is a high-profile game, no?"

"That's different."

"At the risk of sounding cynical, everything's a game," Duff said. "People who adapt will always be ahead."

Bridget pushed her coffee away. "I like the pageant the way it is."

"Me too. But when there's new leadership, all the rules change. Think of it like a safari. Survival of the fittest."

"What are you saying, Duff?"

"Stay alert. Be the lion, not the gazelle."

Closing her eyes, Bridget sighed. "There are worse things than being the gazelle. Like being the hyena. Or the baboon."

"Just be the lion, Bridget," Duff said, grinning. "It's your time to roar."

CHAPTER EIGHT

"It's boring, Mike." Bridget looked around at the stark shoreline of Lake Longmuir, and then back at her long-time rep from the City's Culture and Tourism Department. "Boring."

"It's the beach, Bridget." Mike Delaney looked like he was fighting a grin, but then he usually did. He was a good-natured guy. "How can it be boring?"

"It's the beach of Lake Longmuir, which is no bigger than a puddle. And it's practically winter, Mike. Holding the pageant at the beach would be stupid."

Mike lost the battle with his grin. "Don't hold back. Tell me how you really feel."

The boardwalk running along the beach was unusually quiet, even for a Tuesday morning. An overcast sky and brisk wind were to blame. Without all the hustle and bustle of dogs and their owners, it was just a long stretch of dull.

"I feel like you're setting me up for something, Mike, that's how I feel. Usually I get to choose the pageant site. What gives?"

He guided her along with his hand on her elbow.

That would annoy her with most people, but Mike had become a good pal. Six years earlier, when he was working for a non-profit, he'd competed in the pageant. He lost out on a dog but hooked up with Miguel, who won a bulldog mix, and they all lived happily ever after. When Mike got hired by the City, he'd asked to be assigned to the pageant. His support helped the event grow, and Bridget was grateful. But not grateful enough to take this lying down.

Garbage whirled around them. Fritz, the terrier, raced in circles, trying to catch an empty white plastic bag that flapped like a ghost.

"The beach would be an easy setup," Mike said. "The team-building activity could be a garbage pickup."

"Garbage pickup?" Bridget stopped walking to stare up at him. Mike was at least six foot three, and lanky. "You're thinking pageant participants could show leadership and collaboration skills by collecting trash?"

"Sure, why not? The pageant has always been about showing community spirit."

"You're pulling my leg, right?"

It wouldn't be the first time Mike had pranked her, but today he shook his head. His Adam's apple bobbed twice before he answered. "The beach is only one option."

"I submitted a short list two months ago, and the beach sure as hell wasn't on it." She kicked some pebbles, and Fritz capered after them. He'd been with her nearly constantly since his escape to Sullivan Shaw's house. That little jaunt had been a sign that his training needed fine-tuning. Calling him back, she picked up his leash.

"Your site recommendations were a bit off the beaten path," he said. "City Council preferred something close to the core."

Bridget continued to stare up at him. "Since when did Council get a vote on the pageant site?"

"Since always. They just didn't care to exercise it before now." He glanced toward the street for a moment before adding, "Things are a bit different this year."

"Different how?"

Mike lifted his arm and waved. A tall man in a long black coat waved back from the sidewalk. Then he came across the sand toward them, walking with purposeful grace.

Bridget barely had time to register that it was Mayor Bradshaw before he had joined them. She was a tall woman, but she felt petite between these two giants. Mike made the introductions and the mayor squeezed her hand in a firm political handshake. His hand seemed huge enough to roll a bronze dog on its back and pin it by the throat. Most people probably submitted instantly; Bridget had to fight the urge herself.

"Pleasure to meet you, Bridget." His voice was low and melodious, like a radio announcer's, and his gleaming teeth were the brightest thing on the beach that day. "You're an institution in Dorset Hills."

"Thank you, Mayor." She picked Fritz up and held him out. "This is Fritz, one of the rescue dogs we'll be giving away at the pageant."

"Oh my." The mayor stared at the small dog who was dripping from a dip in the water and covered with slimy green goo. Fritz offered a sandy paw and the mayor took a step backwards and almost tripped off the boardwalk. He recovered with ease, and dusted sand from the nice black wool coat that wasn't designed to be around dogs.

"Sorry, Mayor. He loves people." Bridget set Fritz on the ground, noticing that Beau's tail was at half-mast. Had the mayor wanted to compete in the pageant, he'd be out of luck.

"What an interesting little dog," the mayor said.

He didn't sound interested at all, and when Bridget looked up, he was actually appraising *her* from head to toe with sharp green eyes. She followed his gaze and saw herself through a stranger's eyes. Her boots were covered in sand, slime and dried mud. Her jeans had splotches of red from painting her front door the night before. The paint looked brown on the denim, but on the backs of her hands and under her nails, it looked like dried blood. Then there was the usual old jacket covered in dog hair and slobber. She could barely see through the medusa-like hair whipping into her eyes. At least her mascara wasn't running; she couldn't remember the last time she'd remembered to put some on.

The mayor looked away, as if he'd seen too much. Flames of embarrassment rose from Bridget's chest, crawled up her neck, and started to gnaw at her cheeks. He thought she was one of the crazy dog people, she guessed—the people who didn't care about how they looked anymore. That may be well and good after a certain age, but probably not at 33.

"I must run," Mayor Bradshaw said, checking his watch. "Nice meeting you, Birdie."

He crossed the beach again, picking his way around the empty soda cans and plastic takeout containers.

Bridget waited till there was no chance the wind would carry her words to the mayor's ears. "Mike? What just happened?"

"What do you mean?" His cheeks were flushed, too, under the freckles. His hair was brighter than Duff's—a true ginger.

"Unless I'm much mistaken, I was just erased from existence."

"Oh, Bridget."

"You mean, Birdie."

Mike gave a strangled cough. "I was trying to tell you: things have changed at City Hall."

"Does this guy know about how much money I've brought into this city over the past ten years? The pageant's never had a negative review."

"He was thoroughly briefed, Bridget."

"My track record is impeccable." The wind worked hard to sweep her voice away, so she nearly shouted. "What's with Bill Bradshaw? He may be new to office, but he's not new to Dog Town. I'm sure he's attended previous pageants."

"All I can say is that this mayor marches to his own drummer. Since he's our elected official, we need to march to his drummer, too."

Bridget marched back to the parking lot, and Mike trailed after her.

"You're saying the beach is the mayor's choice?" she asked.

"His *second* choice."

"Let's see his first choice."

BEAU AND FRITZ ran ahead of them up the most popular path in the Dorset Hills Trails system and vanished into the bushes. Trail runs were the only time Beau considered himself off duty and allowed himself to have fun.

The view was spectacular. Since the trees had turned late, the red, orange and yellow leaves still made a gorgeous patchwork quilt that spread out to the neighboring towns and cities squatting among the rolling hills. In another few weeks, every last leaf would be gone, and the scene would be drab until the first snowfall made it pretty again. Bridget had watched many seasons change on these trails.

"Mike, no. A hundred times no."

"But Dorset Hills is all about the trails and the scenery," he said. "It's a way to profile our best assets for the media. We can do the pageant on Clifford's Crest, where there's a natural plateau."

She gave him an incredulous look. "In two weeks, the Crest will be a mudslide. We'll lose the media over the edge, not to mention any seniors who make it this far. Is that your goal? To thin out the city's population? Is it survival of the fittest, now?"

"Very funny. The pageant is one of the most covered—"

"*The* most covered."

"—events of the year. We need to showcase all we have to offer. The mayor was thinking your team activity could be clearing and marking new trails and erecting more plaques."

"I assumed you briefed the mayor about what the trails are like at Thanksgiving? He clearly hasn't muddied his shoes up here."

A couple came around the bend with two dogs cavorting around them. Bridget recognized Remi Malone, a pretty woman she'd turned down for the pageant a few years earlier. Unlike most people, Remi had seemed relieved. She'd been painfully shy then—too shy to survive the competition, although Beau had "passed" her. Today Remi's head was high and her smile wide. That probably had more to do with the beagle parked at her feet than the handsome man holding her hand, Bridget figured. In the end, Remi had found her perfect canine match, as true dog people always did.

Remi stopped and introduced her dog, Leo, even before her boyfriend, Tiller Iverson. Bridget liked a woman who had her priorities in order. She would have chatted longer had Mike not been edging away.

When Remi and Tiller were out of earshot, Mike started the discussion again. "Bridget, this new era will be an adjustment for all of us."

"An adjustment that could ruin the pageant," Bridget said. "I guarantee we'll lose half our audience and a quarter of our participants if the event is held up here. Especially if we get rain and washouts. This makes no sense at all, Mike."

Raking a hand through his ginger hair, he sighed again. "I think Council is going to have to experience that for themselves."

Bridget could tell that his professionalism prevented him from saying more. He was her friend, but he was a city official first. "Mike, there's a lot riding on the success of the pageant this year. More than usual."

He nodded. "Your new house. Your plans to expand your rescue. I know, Bridget. I think we'll just need to work hard and work smart, and we can still pull it off. If we look like team players, I'm sure I can get more funds from the City for setup." Looking around, he added, "And safety rails."

She strode ahead of him to Clifford's Crest, and then spun around, with her arms outstretched. "The Hills are alive... with the sound of my career crashing in ruins."

"You're being a little dramatic. It's one minor setback."

"What's wrong with this mayor? Is he an idiot, or an ass?"

Perching on the edge of a plaque that celebrated Dorset

Hills' history, Mike crossed his arms. "May I speak as your friend for a moment?"

"Shoot." Her arms were still outstretched. "Shoot me now."

"Bridget, with this mayor, you'll catch more flies with honey."

"I don't need to suck up because I do good work."

"In the political realm, sometimes you need to do good work *and* offer honey. It hasn't been a big issue in Dog Town before. Now, we just need to adapt. I've been asked to find a way to glitz up the pageant a bit."

"Glitz! This is bull—"

Mike raised a hand to silence her. Another couple had come up the trail and reached the plateau. This time Mike opened the conversation. "Hey, Sullivan," he called.

Bridget's new neighbor was standing next to a slender woman in yoga gear. Sullivan looked significantly less slick than usual, in hiking boots, a green rain jacket and a baseball cap. She was pleased that he was just run-of-the-mill handsome, instead of stunningly so. His good looks annoyed her.

Sullivan smirked at Bridget's outstretched arms. "Sound of Music, right? Is it a free show?"

She set her hands on her hips. "Only for friends."

"Well, we're neighbors. Next best thing." He turned to his companion. "Bridget, this is Grace."

Grace held out a delicate hand and offered Bridget a smile.

"Grace, of course." Her hand felt like a limp dead bird in Bridget's. "Sorry, I didn't recognize you out of context." Turning to Mike, she explained, "I know Grace from Boners."

"Boners?" Sullivan asked.

"Bone Appetit Bistro," Grace said. "Bridget's a waitress there."

"And Grace is one of my regulars," Bridget said. "How's Chico doing?"

Bridget had turned Grace down for a rescue dog the previous Thanksgiving, partly because the little townhouse she rented looked like a museum. A collection of antique dolls sat on shelves in every room. It had creeped Bridget out a little, but more practically, it didn't seem like the right place for dogs that loved nothing more than dirty trail runs. She'd suggested that Grace would do better with a gentle Havanese. Instead, Grace had subsequently gotten a Chihuahua, a huge dog in small packaging. She'd seen Chico lunging at a wolfhound once; small though he was, he'd nearly pulled Grace over. It was a self-made match gone wrong.

Grace's face flushed. She was quite pretty, but so slight that you didn't notice it immediately. "Chico lives with my aunt, now."

Bridget changed the subject. "Beautiful day, isn't it?"

"Not really," Sullivan said. "But it beats mud season. I hear we're getting a foot of rain this weekend. That'll bring the leaves down."

Bridget gave Mike a pointed look. "Yes. Yes, it will."

Suddenly, Beau and Fritz came tearing back down the trail. Seeing Sullivan and Grace, Beau slammed on his brakes. He came to stop beside Bridget, whereas Fritz careened on and launched himself at Sullivan's chest. Grace screamed as the dog sent Sullivan reeling back a few paces. Still, he managed to catch the terrier.

"I'm so sorry," Bridget said, running over. "Fritz, what's gotten into you?"

Fritz was licking Sullivan's face. Bridget expected him

to drop the dog, but he didn't. Instead, he wiped his cheek with one sleeve, grinning. "I showered already today, buddy, but thanks."

Bridget tried to grab Fritz, but Sullivan was holding the dog out to Grace. "Isn't this one cute?"

Grace backed away with her palms up. "Adorable."

Bridget sheepishly collected the terrier. Fritz had left muddy paw prints all over Sullivan's jacket, and his face glistened with dog slobber.

"All the dogs have fallen back a bit since we moved," she said, glancing at Mike. "Change is upsetting for them. But we're doubling down on training before the pageant."

"I'm sure they'll be perfect as usual," Mike said. "What breed is Fritz?"

"Cairn terrier mostly. With a titch of Brittany and a smidge of schnauzer."

"A titch?" Sullivan said, smirking again.

"About five per cent, according to his DNA test," she said.

"You DNA tested the dog? That's gotta be a scam."

"I use every means possible to understand my dogs better. The bouncy bit comes from the Brittany."

"The smidge, you mean."

"The titch, actually." She gave him a chilly smile. "Mock me all you like. The science of dog rescue is too complicated for most people."

"She's joking, Sullivan," Mike said.

"No, she isn't. But that's okay. She takes her work very seriously."

"I most certainly do," Bridget said.

Mike turned to Sullivan and Grace. "What do you think about this as a site for the pageant?"

"Perfect," Grace said, without a moment's hesitation.

Sullivan took a good look around before answering. "I don't know. You need a stage, right? How are you going to get everything up here and stable?"

Bridget began, "That's—"

"A valid point I'll take back to Council," Mike said.

Bridget released Fritz and he hurled himself once again into Sullivan's arms. The dog clearly had a crush. It wasn't going over well with Grace, if her look of mild disgust was any indication. Otherwise, they seemed like a good match, Bridget thought. Sullivan looked like a Ken doll and Grace was Ballerina Barbie.

Sullivan set Fritz on the ground again, and said, "You know what site *would* work well for the pageant? The beach. Easy access, right near the core."

Mike now gave Bridget a pointed look, and she felt her hackles rising.

"You and the mayor think alike, Sullivan," Mike said.

"Good to know," Sullivan said, smiling. "Because Bill and I are having lunch later this week. I'll cast my vote for the boardwalk."

Bridget turned without another word and started down the trail. Beau was glued to her side, as always, but Fritz had to be called away from Sullivan several times. Each repetition sounded less musical and more manic. Sullivan annoyed her more than a smidge or a titch, and Grace was welcome to him.

CHAPTER NINE

The single best moment of Bridget's day was coming home to a warm greeting from a happy pack of dogs. When she felt like she'd been dissed by the City, and undervalued at the bistro, 13 wagging tails did much to soothe her soul. Now that those tails wagged in her very own home, it felt like Thanksgiving every night.

On top of that, one of her friends was usually at hand either to work on the house, or work on the dogs. This evening, Nika had come over after her shift at the vet clinic to tend to a small sore on the hind end of Percy the Portuguese waterdog cross. After that, she examined 12 sets of teeth, 24 eyes, and 24 ears. As their official debut date neared, they couldn't afford any issues, especially visible ones. Appearances had always counted where the dogs were concerned. Now that appeared to extend to their handler, as well.

"What's wrong, Bee?" Nika asked, smoothing Lulu's rough coat. "You're awfully quiet."

Bridget slouched on a wood chair at the kitchen table. "November is so draining. If I had my druthers, I'd probably only leave this house to walk the dogs. Yet most days I'm out poking around strangers' homes or meeting sponsors. Then I run myself ragged waiting tables. On top of all that, this year I have a mayor who wants nothing to do with me, yet still wants to micromanage the pageant."

Nika looked like she wished she hadn't asked—probably not because she didn't care, but because she didn't know what to say. Duff was usually the one to handle Bridget's pre-pageant jitters.

"It'll all work out fine," Nika said, sitting down in the middle of the kitchen floor and crossing her legs. "It always does, doesn't it?"

"I guess so." Bridget dragged Beau over to get inspected, too. He submitted like a gentleman, although he hated having his ears sniffed.

Nika finished with Beau and pulled Fritz into position. Her eyes lost focus as she started going over his coat. She knew the geography of these dogs by memory, and it was easiest to let her fingertips search for trouble. One by one, she groped every dog from head to toe, looking for ticks, sores, and miscellaneous bumps. Keeping tabs on that many dogs was a big job.

When she was nearly done, Bridget asked, "Tea or wine?"

Nika pretended to think about the question as Bridget crossed to the wine rack. Maisie and Cori rarely touched alcohol, so it was nice to unwind with Nika. When she finished with the last dog, Nika let them surge all over her, wriggling and licking, before taking the glass Bridget handed her.

Still on the floor, Nika raised her glass. "To the best pageant ever."

As they sipped, there was a knock on the front door.

The dogs exploded into barking, only to be instantly silenced as Bridget called, "Quiet." They'd done their job. Only a foolish visitor would get up to funny business with 13 dogs on the premises.

She opened the front door to find a tall, earnest-looking man with closely cropped fair hair and a serious set to his square jaw standing on the porch. The sun was setting behind him but there was enough light to see he was wearing a uniform of some kind.

"Good evening, Ms. Linsmore," he said, flashing a badge that she could barely see. "I'm Officer Moller. Joe Moller."

"Hello, Officer. What can I do for you?" Bridget didn't open the screen, for 13 good reasons. Fritz couldn't see out the door, or even push through the pack to get near it, so he just jumped again and again to try to get a look at the man.

"We've had a complaint, ma'am," he said.

"A complaint?" She was irked by the "ma'am." He looked about her age, after all. "What kind of complaint?"

He cleared his throat. "A complaint that there are too many dogs on the premises, ma'am."

Bridget fumbled on the wall for the switch and Officer Moller blinked a few times as the light came on. There was a City crest on his dark jacket, but the uniform wasn't familiar. "Someone called the cops about my dogs?"

"Not the police, ma'am." He cleared his throat again; it must be a nervous tic. "The Canine Corrections Department."

"You're a dog cop?" Her voice rose enough to cause a ripple in the pack. Beau forced his way through the throng and pressed against her side.

Nika came out of the kitchen with her wine glass. "What's going on?"

"A dog cop is here with a complaint about the number of dogs on the premises."

"Why?" Nika nudged dogs aside with her knee so she could stand beside Bridget.

He raised his phone and read from the screen. "City bylaw subsection five point two prescribes that residential home owners may have up to four dogs on the premises."

"Excuse me?" Bridget sounded confused. All the words made sense, but what he said didn't compute. "I don't understand."

"I'm saying you have too many dogs here, ma'am." He cleared his throat. "According to City bylaws."

"Too many dogs? That's ridiculous!" Bridget's words shot out. "Since when is there a limit on how many dogs people can have?"

Officer Moller stepped back, as if Bridget's tone was more daunting than 13 dogs trying to get at him through a screen door. "It's the same bylaw that's been around for 20 years, ma'am. Nothing's changed."

"Something's changed, because I usually have more than four dogs, and dog cops have never come by."

His shrug was almost imperceptible. "The only thing that's changed is that someone complained, ma'am. I guess no one did before. So, now we had to come out."

Nika reached behind Bridget and turned out the lights. "Okay, you came out. How many dogs do you see, Officer?"

"Very funny, but I'm not the one drinking," he said. "Rough head count, a dozen dogs, give or take."

"Who complained?" Bridget asked.

"I'm not at liberty to say, ma'am. The CCD has an anonymous hotline."

Bridget turned the light back on, and then squeezed out

the door past the dogs. Beau whined, but she shushed him. "Is this for real? Or is someone pranking me?"

Nika's fingers were busy on her phone. "He's right about the City bylaws, Bridget. But I see no mention of their ever being enforced."

"Someone's gotta be pranking me. It's Frank, I bet."

Officer Moller shook his head. "It's not a prank, ma'am. I'm sorry."

She stared at him, looking for clues. "If you're with the CCD you must know who I am."

"I know about your rescue work and the pageant, ma'am, yes."

Every "ma'am" felt like a smack. "Let's cut to the chase, Officer Moller. Who do I have to talk to clear this up?"

"You can call the CCD in the morning ma'am. You'll also need to remove eight or so dogs to get under the legal limit."

"After the Thanksgiving pageant, I'll be down to one dog."

"Ma'am—"

Bridget raised her hand. "Stop calling me that. I'm not your grandmother, Dog Officer Joe."

He took another step backwards. One more and he'd fall down the stairs.

"Sorry, uh, miss. I'm authorized to seize the excess dogs tonight if I need to." He gestured to the City van parked behind him. "We'll impound them at Animal Services until you make arrangements."

All the air came out of Bridget's lungs all at once in a choking gasp. "No! You can't touch my dogs." There was a rolling growl behind her, deep in Beau's chest.

Officer Moller turned and jumped down the stairs. From the bottom, he asked, "Are you threatening me, miss?"

"That would be one of the dogs you're thinking of removing," she said. "Nika, phone, please. I'm calling the real cops."

Nika slipped through the door and handed over her phone. Then she went down the stairs and approached Office Moller. "Is all this fuss necessary?" she asked. "You can see the dogs are all well behaved. The only one that growled is Bridget's personal dog and he's protective."

"I have my orders to—"

"Investigate, right? And make a judgement call, I'm sure." Nika looked up at him. "Can't you just issue a warning and give Bridget time to deal with the situation herself? You'd be upset too if neighbors were complaining just days after you moved in."

"Well, it would mean—"

"I'm the veterinary assistant to these dogs, and I can speak to their good nature. They barely barked when you knocked. Do you know how rare that is, Officer Joe?"

"They seem nice enough. Except for the big black one. But the bylaw is clear."

Nika moved around him slowly, and he turned too. "I'm sure you have some flexibility. Especially when Bridget's never had a single complaint about her dogs in over ten years. Lots of people in Dog Town have more than four dogs, Joe. They come into the vet's office with six or eight at a time. It's on record."

Joe Moller shifted uneasily. He hadn't prepared for all this. "Maybe they have a kennel license."

"I doubt that very much. People normally get a vet's reference for that. I can only remember a few breeders coming in with the form."

"Then I guess no one's complained about their dogs."

Nika persisted. "I know for a fact that people complain

to the CCD hotline all the time, especially about barking. So then the owners come into the vet all upset and want us to put their dogs on tranquillizers."

"Tranquillizers?" Joe's eyebrows went up.

"We get at least two requests a week, I kid you not. Obviously, we can't tranquillize all the dogs who bark in Dorset Hills, Joe."

He looked confused now. "We're getting off course."

Nika pressed her case. "I'm just saying that all dogs bark and putting them on medication would send a terrible message to the public about Dorset Hills. Think about the headlines: 'Dog Town Dogs Doped.'"

Bridget came to stand beside her. "I would never dope my dogs."

Nika grabbed Bridget's arm to silence her. "*You* wouldn't, but think about all the people who would. I'm in a position to know just how many ill-informed owners would go to extreme measures to keep their dogs quiet... just to keep their dogs."

"I hate to think that, but you're probably right," Bridget said. "I met the mayor yesterday, and it seems like he really cares about appearances and Dorset Hills' image. So maybe you folks at the CCD need to think this through a little bit more, Joe. It could backfire."

"Our mission is to keep dogs safe and residents happy," he said.

"A worthy goal," Nika said. "I'm just saying if people get scared about losing their dogs, they might do desperate, crazy things. Things that end up on the news."

"Not me, of course," Bridget said. "I have full confidence that the City will support upstanding dog owners." She knelt beside Beau and put an arm around his neck. "Just the thought of seeing his face looking out of a cage..."

"Don't even say it," Nika said. "We'd organize a sit-in and invite every newspaper in the country. What was the magazine that did that first story on Dorset Hills? The one that launched it as the dog capital of North America?"

"*Luxe and Leisure*," Bridget said. "I keep in touch with the writer. She plans to come for next year's pageant."

With every comment, Joe had taken another step back toward the City van. Finally, he said, "If you'll excuse me, I'm just going to call—"

"It's getting late," Nika said. "Let's deal with this tomorrow when everyone's fresh. You've done what you came to do, which was alert Bridget to a complaint from neighbors."

"Sullivan Shaw," Bridget muttered. "That—"

Nika shushed her. "It's obviously upsetting when you've just moved into a new home and find people are complaining. But you've given us a lot to think about." She walked after Joe. "Just so that I understand correctly, Officer, you're saying that people need a kennel license to keep more than four dogs on the premises."

"According to municipal bylaws, yes."

"Then I guess Bridget will need to apply for one."

"I wouldn't wait too long," he said.

Bridget hurried after him. "Are you threatening me, Joe?"

He rushed the last few steps to his van. "Of course not, ma'am."

Nika finally caught his arm and he slowed, and turned. "Tell us what you mean, Officer." She looked up at him with her big amber eyes and his expression softened.

"The CCD looks at complaints before issuing a kennel license. Ms. Linsmore is one down already. Red flagged."

He eased his sleeve out of Nika's grip and climbed into the van.

Bridget held the door so he couldn't close it. "Wait. I bought this place to have a kennel. To expand. Are you telling me one neighbor can ruin everything I've worked for just by calling your hotline?"

"Let go, please." Joe tugged on the door. "You'll want to contact the licensing department. I'm just the field officer."

"What kind of complaints count against me?" Bridget pressed.

"Anything dog-related. Numbers, nuisance, you name it."

He pulled hard on the door and Bridget held on, her fingers whitening from the effort. "How many, Joe? How many complaints does it take to wreck my chances?"

Finally, he pried off her fingers one by one. He yanked the door closed and shouted through the closed window. "Three strikes and you're out, ma'am."

CHAPTER TEN

"Bridget?"
    "Bridget?"
  "Bridget!"

So many customers were calling her name that Bridget couldn't figure out who to serve first. She'd been up most of the night worrying and the Boners breakfast crowd had never been so demanding and annoying.

"What's wrong with people today?" she said to Rachel, grabbing a fresh pot of coffee.

"They're used to your coddling and you're neglecting them today," she said. "Grace has only had one hot water refill. That teabag has plenty left to give."

Bridget forced a smile, but it felt as if her face might crack under the strain. "I'll get right on that. At least she tips. Unlike Gerry."

Rachel's section filled up slower and yet her tips were usually double Bridget's. "You've backed yourself into a corner, Bee," she said. "Everyone you've ever turned down for a dog wants to sit in your section and make you pay for wounding their ego. And you feel so guilty you overcompensate. It's a vicious cycle that can only end one way."

Pouring a couple of inches of coffee into a mug, Bridget ignored the rumblings behind her and downed it in a shot. "What way is that?"

"By promoting yourself to manager and easing Frank into retirement."

Bridget stared at Rachel, her mouth still hanging open. "What?"

"Don't tell me you haven't thought about it."

"I *haven't* thought about it. I've got my hands full as it is."

"Managing Boners will be less work than what you're doing now. Hire a couple of new staff."

The chorus behind them got louder. Grace's quiet plea somehow pierced the guys' grumbling.

Bridget held up an index finger to let them know she'd heard. "Frank said he'd leave here in a pine box."

"No one begrudges him a dramatic exit," Rachel said. "But until then he can sit in a booth and drink coffee from a bottomless cup."

Bridget laughed. "No free refills when I'm in charge."

Rachel hoisted her tray of breakfast specials high and started gliding toward her tables. "That's the spirit."

"And no one calls it Boners, either," Bridget called after her.

"Good luck with that," Rachel called back.

Bridget filled a teapot with hot water, grabbed another teabag and then hurried over to Grace's table. "Sorry for the wait, Grace. Fresh teabag on the house."

Grace dunked the bag twice and pulled it out of the pot. "Thanks. And I'm sorry if Sullivan upset you the other day, Bridget. He just blurts things, sometimes."

"No worries. And I'm sorry I brought up Chico. I didn't realize it hadn't worked out. Chihuahuas are—"

Grace cut her off. "It was best for all concerned."

"Of course. Guys like Sullivan tend not to like teacup dogs."

Pouring a teaspoon of skim milk into her pale tea, Grace clattered as she stirred. Then she added a microscopic amount of her sugar substitute and stirred again. "I suppose not."

She stared up at Bridget with hazel eyes. No wonder Sullivan liked Grace. A frail little thing would activate his inner hero. If he had one.

"Are you two dating or something?" a voice said behind them.

"Oh, Trent," Bridget said, as she turned. "There's enough of me to go around."

"Well, we're parched and suffering today, Bee. What's going on?"

She grabbed the coffee pot out of Rachel's hand as she passed and then filled Trent's empty cup. "What do you know about the Canine Corrections Department?"

Trent rolled his eyes. "Cop wannabes. They can't keep staff because they're all putting in time till they can become real cops."

"What's changed lately? I never knew the CCD to do much except pick up strays."

"Manager's getting cocky," Trent said, furrowing his bushy grey eyebrows. "Cliff Whorley. He's a retired state trooper with delusions of grandeur, from what I hear. Need me to talk to him?"

"Not at all," Bridget said. "Just curious."

"Can you get curious about our empty cups?"

Four off-duty firefighters were grinning when she

turned. "Oh, boys, you are way too big for one booth," she said, hoping flirtation would soothe egos. It always worked for Duff.

"Flattery will get you everywhere," said Ron, the chattiest firefighter, as she poured the last of the coffee into his cup. "You let us know if you need help with the dog cops, Bee."

By the time she got back to the counter, Bridget's smile felt more genuine. It faded quickly, however, when she saw the tall, ginger-haired man perched on her usual stool. "What are you doing here, Mike?"

"Sit." He patted the stool next to him. "I heard about what happened."

"With the dog cop? Could you believe it? I hope you're handling it."

He stared at her. "I'm here to handle you."

"Me? I got accosted in my home by a dog cop who threatened to take my dogs away."

"And you threatened to call national media, if his report is correct." Mike didn't wait for her response. "I can tell from your expression that it is."

"That was Nika. But the guy was an ass."

"He was doing his job. Do you think he wanted to come out there and tell you that?" Sighing, Mike ran one hand through his red hair. "Like I said, Bee, things are changing. You have to be more—I don't know—tactful?"

"Strategic is the word you want."

They looked up to see another redhead. Duff had overheard at least part of the conversation.

"That word would do nicely, Andrea," Mike said. "Great to see you."

"Call me Duff. You're the only one in Dog Town who doesn't."

"You just don't look like a Duff to me."

"She looks like a Duff to us," one of the firefighters called.

"Easy boys," she called. "Maybe I'll let you buy me a coffee later."

Bridget saw how that was going and called, "No 'bottomless' jokes, guys. This is my best friend."

Bridget glanced at Grace's table and found she'd left before getting her next two refills. Hopefully she'd still tipped, because every cent counted these days.

"Bee." Duff tapped her shoulder. "Mike and I are worried about you. He's confirming the scuttlebutt I heard about City Council getting more antsy and controlling."

Mike stood and shook Duff's hand, as if to signal a passing of the torch. "Gotta run. Talk soon."

Bridget watched him go before facing Duff. "Go easy, please. I'm upset as it is."

Duff's blue eyes were sympathetic. "You've got to soften those edges, Bee."

"I wouldn't know how to begin."

"You do it here all the time," Duff said. "Your customers love you."

Glancing around, Bridget sighed. "That's different."

"Why? It's like you have one rule here, and another for everywhere else."

It was true, Bridget realized. She felt safe at the bistro and always had. No matter how tiring and frustrating the work, it was her turf. Everywhere else it felt like she had a target on her back, so she'd developed a thick skin. Obviously, it came off the wrong way.

Sighing, she rested her head in her hands. "What do you want me to do, Duff?"

Her friend patted her shoulder. "Let me think about it,

and we'll talk when there aren't so many distractions. For now, all you need to do is be nice."

"Be nice? I'd rather stab my eyes out with a dull knife." She grabbed one off the counter for emphasis, and Duff pressed her hand down.

Voices rose behind her.

"Be right there, Trent," she called. "Hang tight."

"See how easy that was?" Duff asked. "All you need to do is spread that sunshine around."

Bridget got up and grabbed her tray. "Why do I get the feeling I'm in for a makeover?"

Duff laughed. "They're not just for dogs anymore."

A BARE BRANCH snapped out of Bridget's hand and nearly hit Nika in the face. "Sorry, Nika," she said, forging on along the narrow path through the woods. In summer this trail had probably been almost impenetrable, but it had thinned now.

"Bee, this is a bad idea," Nika said. "It'll be dark soon and— Oh darn, burrs! Do not bring the other dogs out here. Maisie will kill you if they get burred."

Bridget pulled Beau closer to keep him on the path. "It'll be fine. We'll keep this short and sweet. I'll be nice, just like Duff ordered."

"No way Duff sanctioned this visit. Not buying it." Nika yanked her coat out of the bushes. "Ouch. Thorns. Is there a reason we couldn't just take the car?"

"Element of surprise. I'm the lion, Nika." Bridget tripped over a root and made a nice recovery. "See? I always land on my paws."

Nika snorted. "What's with the safari talk?"

"It's survival of the fittest, Duff said. She told me to be the lion, not the gazelle."

"But she also told you to be nice? I'm not sure I'm following." Nika was puffing from trying to keep up over the rough terrain.

Bridget glanced over her shoulder and smiled. "It's complicated. For now, we're being nice on the outside and fierce on the inside. That's how I'm interpreting it."

"Well, I'm guessing Duff would have wanted to supervise this safari. But it looks like we're here now."

The trail widened slightly and then spit them out onto a long driveway. At the bottom was a house similar to Bridget's but painted a sunny yellow. She scowled at the sleek sportscar parked near the door of the rustic cottage. It belonged downtown with the new condo he was developing along Lake Longmuir. When she interviewed him two years ago, he'd lived in that area.

Walking down the driveway, she saw the place was well kept. The gardens were filled with orange and yellow chrysanthemums, and a rake stood against a shed beside bags of leaves. A wheelbarrow filled with logs sat by the stairs. There was even a harvest wreath on the door. Why would he bother with all that if he wanted to knock down both their houses and build something huge and completely at odds with the neighborhood?

Beau's tail dropped with every step until it practically dusted the wood on the deck. "I couldn't agree more, pal," Bridget said.

"Pardon me?" Nika asked.

"Oh, nothing." Bridget opened the screen door and used the brass doorknocker shaped like a hound's head. Once. Twice. Three times. She was going for a fourth when the door swung open.

"Hey." Sullivan Shaw stood in the open doorway. His hair was unruly and his sweatpants baggy, yet he somehow managed to look better than ever. "Here to borrow a cup of sugar? How sweet."

Nika laughed a little too hard at this and Bridget elbowed her into silence.

"I don't have time for baking these days," Bridget said. Her heart was still beating hard from the walk. She must be getting out of shape.

"Sorry to hear that." He leaned out and checked for her car. "You walked through the bush to talk about cupcakes?"

"Actually, no." She took a deep breath and met his eyes. "I walked through the bush to ask why you called the CCD on me."

His brow furrowed. "And the CCD is...?"

"The Canine Corrections Department. As if you don't know."

Leaning against the doorframe, he crossed his arms. "So you think I called animal services because Fritz tipped my garbage? Wouldn't that be an overreaction?"

"It most certainly would be. I was surprised that you did."

"And now you can be surprised that I didn't."

"The dog cop said a neighbor complained and you're the closest one. And the only one who's even met me."

Now Sullivan offered his annoying smirk. "I imagine you've annoyed a few people in Dog Town, Bridget. I can't be the only one."

"You're the only one with—"

"A real bone to pick? Possibly. But I managed to cope with picking up my trash, and even with Fritz assaulting me in the hills."

"Fritz assaulted him?" Nika asked.

"He likes him. Good grief."

Sullivan's teeth flashed. "There's no accounting for taste, I guess."

Bridget looked away. His smile was an unwelcome distraction. "Look, I just want you to know that calling the CCD could ruin my hopes for expanding my business."

Nika moved closer and gave Bridget a warning pinch. But the damage was already done.

Sullivan pushed himself upright and filled the doorway. "Expanding how?"

Bridget tried to correct course. "I just want my pageant to get bigger and better every year, that's all. Having the CCD breathing down my neck isn't going to help."

"I'd only have reason to call them if your dogs were a nuisance. Well, *more* of a nuisance. Fritz is okay, but this big guy is just—"

"Wait, don't—" Nika began.

"Creepy," Sullivan finished.

"Excuse me?" Bridget's voice was low, and Beau's growl underscored it.

"Make that menacing," Sullivan said.

"You wouldn't know a great dog if—"

"It bit me? I hope it doesn't come to that."

"Bridget, that's enough. Your lion is showing." Nika grabbed her friend's elbow and pulled her away. "It was nice seeing you, Sullivan. Thanks for not calling the CCD."

"Oh, he called," Bridget said, as Nika towed her down the stairs. "He wants me out of that house so he can take over."

"Oh, Bridget, move on," he said. "I have."

Bridget resisted, and Beau took little jumps at Nika but she kept her grip till they got to the path.

"Both of you stop it and be gazelles," Nika said. "Or he really will call the CCD."

Sullivan came out to the steps in bare feet, laughing as they wrestled. "Thanks for the show. It's like 'Wild Kingdom' or something."

"Big picture, Bridget. Big picture," Nika said, urging her friend on with little shoves in the shoulder. "One day you'll have a nice kennel in that barn and forty rescue dogs. If we have to bake Sullivan Shaw cupcakes to get there, that is what we shall do."

"Never. I have pride, Nika."

"Lions have prides, right? Let's talk about that."

CHAPTER ELEVEN

Training Day, the first public event leading up to the pageant, was always nerve-wracking, but never more than this year. Now, in addition to worrying about all the things that could go wrong with a cast of furry characters, Bridget worried for the first time about the people. Specifically, with Mayor Bradshaw scheduled to attend, she worried he'd be judging her, when this day was supposed to be all about her judging everyone else.

"A perfect Saturday afternoon," Duff said. "Let's hope everything else goes to plan."

"I've got a bad feeling about this," Bridget said, as she helped Cori set up plastic barriers in the sunny south corner of Seaton Dog Park. "I don't know why."

"Performance anxiety," Duff said. "Looks like we're going to have a big crowd."

People had started gathering early, and Bridget scanned the crowd for familiar faces. Trent and a couple of the firefighters from Boners were already there. Remi and Tiller waved from a picnic table, where they were sitting so close together a breeze couldn't squeeze through. Tonna

Rafferty, who ran Beta Dogs, an upscale doggie day care, headed toward Cori to lend a hand. Bridget didn't love all of Cori's friends, but Tonna was funny and surprisingly elegant for someone who supervised a pack for a living. Even Arianna Torrance, a stunning blonde dog breeder, had shown up. They didn't know each other well, but Bridget recognized a kindred spirit when she met one: Ari was as attached to her large poodle hybrid as Bridget was to Beau.

"This has to be double the size of last year's crowd," Bridget said.

"Everything will be fine, Bee," Cori said, pushing six leashes into her hand. "We've got your back."

Bridget nodded, and focussed on the dogs. That always worked to ground her. In this case, however, the six dogs were all graduates from Cori's personal training program, and needed little attention. So, she appraised the park instead. It was new, huge and little more than a fenced patch of land. After years of pressure from the Seaton Neighborhood Committee, the former mayor had granted permission for the build just before he left office. Seaton had never felt much love from City Hall before. It had been one of the rougher neighborhoods since long before Dorset Hills became Dog Town. In fact, the dog-crazy sentiment hadn't penetrated here as it had elsewhere. While there were plenty of dog owners, Bridget suspected they had more to worry about than luxury dog care and accoutrements.

"This space is perfect," Nika said, as she joined them. "There's room for a crowd and yet the dogs are completely safe."

"It's safe, but it doesn't have the glitz factor Mike said the mayor wants," Bridget said.

Cori rolled her eyes before kneeling to release the dogs one by one. "Glitz? Really?"

"Politicians care about optics," Duff said, lifting her eyes from the iPad she was using to keep track of the agenda. "And this place is nothing but fenced dirt."

Cori stood, bristling. "That's why I proposed it. This event will bring attention to an area that really needs it."

Bridget tried to do that with every pageant. It hadn't started off as a crusade but evolved that way. Somehow it seemed fitting to hold her events in neighborhoods that truly embraced mutts. There was scarcely a purebred to be seen in Seaton. Yet the local dogs deserved a great place to run.

"I know, Cori, and personally, I agree with you," Duff said. "But it's last year's thinking. We're in a new era now."

Cori made a face. "This new era sucks."

"It was too late to find another training site anyway," Bridget said. "It's bad enough that we have to hold the pageant in the hills. Honestly."

"Yeah, I'm not sold on the hills," Duff said. "Leave that to me, Bee. I'm going to try charming the mayor today."

"Good luck with that." Catching herself, Bridget grinned slyly. "I mean, if anyone could do it, you can, Duff. You look great today."

"Nice save," Duff said, grinning back. "Don't waste the sweet talk on me. Save it for the mayor."

"If he actually acknowledges I exist, I will do my best. Am I the lion or the gazelle today? Nika and I were struggling with the analogy the other day."

Duff rolled her eyes. "I'll play dumb to your stupid, Bee. The idea of being a lion is simply to stay in the game and compete like you mean it. Being nice is one tactic for winning."

"Fake," Cori said. "Fake-ity fake fake fake."

"Smart," Duff countered. "And that's why Bridget put me in charge of strategy."

Cori's sharp brown eyes widened. "Seriously, Bee? Duff doesn't know dogs."

"Duff knows people," Bridget said. "You and I know dogs, but that's not enough anymore. We're in a whole new dog park, Cori. Part of being a good leader is recognizing what you don't know. And I don't know politics."

"It's just a matter of carving up the work to suit our skills," Duff said. "Cori, your training demos are always a huge hit. Now you can focus only on that. Bridget can focus on selecting the final contenders. Nika can manage the spectators, and Maisie can help keep things organized while I manage the VIPs."

Cori sniffed disdainfully. "We used to be above this sort of bull—"

Duff interrupted. "Keep an eye on the long game. If this goes well, you get to rescue and train more abandoned dogs. Bridget gets to have the kennel she's always wanted. And I get to see my friends succeed at their dreams."

Bridget gave Cori a pleading look. "I trust Duff's judgement in this, Cori, just as I trust yours where training is concerned. Now, go do what you do best."

"Fine," Cori said, heading off to the opposite corner, where Tonna and a couple of others had erected a hay bale enclosure.

Nika and Maisie got people settled behind portable barriers, and Duff walked briskly to the center of the park with Bridget.

"Welcome to the ninth annual pre-pageant event," Duff called. "I'm Andrea MacDuff, and you all know Bridget Linsmore." She motioned to Bridget, who took a deep bow as applause swelled. "Today we'll select 24 human finalists for the pageant by putting them through their paces in the training ring. Next week, we'll be back, same time, same place, to reveal the 12 canine finalists. Five days after that, of course, is Thanksgiving and the pageant itself. Make sure you follow us on social media to get the breaking pageant details." She turned with a big smile. "Bridget...?"

"This year's event promises to be the best ever," Bridget said. "Honestly, the thought of parting with these 12 dogs makes me very sad—and happy for 12 of you. We're putting the final touches on them now. I'm eager to see how you do in the training ring today with the demonstration dogs. Don't be nervous. We're not looking for expert skills—just a good attitude and that special something that sets true dog lovers apart."

Duff gestured with a flourish toward the hay bales. "We have a surprise today. Cori Hogan, our pro trainer, is going to show off her skills with her border collie, Clem. Few of us will reach this pinnacle of connection with our dogs, but it shows us what's possible."

A huge cheer went up and Bridget and Duff moved behind the barricade with the contestants.

Cori kicked down the hay bales and released three sheep into the park. They ran out and gathered in the center. Cori came after them with Clem, her black-and-white border collie. He was the smartest dog Bridget had ever encountered, and the best trained. In the past three years, Cori and Clem had travelled to herding competitions all over the country and brought back a dozen trophies. She had never thought to exploit this talent... but Duff had.

With a series of whistles and hand gestures, Cori led Clem to maneuver the sheep around the dog park, taking them past the audience. There were oohs and aahs and cheers, none of which fazed Clem in the least. He had a job to do and he did it superbly, becoming a small black-and-white blur, up, down, circling, dodging left and right, a little nip here and there, to keep the sheep moving in the right direction. By the time the show was over, the sheep were back in the enclosure and the hay bales went up again. Cori threw down a bale, hopped on top with Clem and did a sweeping bow. The applause was deafening.

"You're a freaking genius," Bridget told Duff.

"Tell me that *after* Thanksgiving," she said.

A 'pit crew' composed of the Rescue Mafia and half a dozen others quickly moved barriers to make a pen in the middle of the dog park. Nika and Maisie lined up nearly forty pageant contestants and brought six forward. One of them was Trixie Dayton, Beau's favorite. She bounced on her toes from excitement.

Meanwhile, Cori brought over the demonstration dogs from their pen. They were as calm and cool as the ponies hired out for kids' parties. Bombproof. Most were retriever crosses, and it was no wonder so many with these genes made great service dogs.

In the ring, Cori handed a leash to each contestant. Trixie stopped bouncing the second the leash was in her hand. The brown Lab mix licked her hand and then sat watching Cori. For the next 20 minutes, they pretty much went in circles, stopping and starting, using the hand gestures Cori showed them to get the dogs to sit, lie down and walk nicely. They put the dogs in a down stay and walked around them. Finally, they summoned their demo dog by name, and offered liver treats and hugs. The leashes went back into Cori's hands, and she bowed again.

"Perfectly choreographed," Duff whispered to Bridget. "She's very good when she isn't being a pain in the butt."

"Aren't we all?" Bridget said. She shook the hands of the first contestants and signalled the next six to come in.

This time the dog Trixie had been paired with was assigned to Jonah Barnes. He had a boyishly handsome face and handled the dog with the same steady earnestness that Trixie had. Somewhere in the back of Bridget's mind a little bell rang. Jonah and Trixie seemed like a good fit. She'd make sure they worked together at Cori's classroom training session the next week.

After the third group finished, they took a break. Duff led Bridget over to the VIP area, where Mike was waiting with about a dozen sponsors.

"Hey, this is going great," he said. "The sheep were an excellent touch. The photographer for the *Expositor* just left, so I think we'll get some play in tomorrow's paper."

"Not to mention social media," Duff said. "Did you see all the cell phones waving? People love smart dog videos almost as much as dumb dog videos."

Bridget looked around. "Where's the mayor?"

Mike's smile faded. "I'm sorry, Bee. He had other pressing business."

"Other business? Mike, the sitting mayor always comes to training day. And debut day. Then he announces the matches at the pageant. It's tradition."

He patted Bridget's arm. "I'm sure he'll be here next week. Don't read too much into this, Bee. He'll see the coverage and be very impressed, I'm sure of it."

Bridget's shoulders slumped. "He dissed me."

"Hush," Duff said. "The show must go on, Bee. We have sponsors to woo."

Bridget followed Duff as they circulated among the sponsors, shaking hands. Finally, Mike introduced them to a man Bridget had never met.

"This is Dave Hedley. He's owns the franchise for Build Right, which is set to open next month."

Build Right had previously been shut out of Dorset Hills by the old guard lest they take business away from shops owned by longstanding citizens, like Hound's Tooth Hardware. The fact that the huge store got a tract of land originally promised to a seniors' center was indeed a sign that times were changing.

Dave seemed like a nice guy, despite his big box store background, and was quick to tell Bridget he owned a rescue dog himself—a border collie mix.

"I couldn't believe that show with the sheep," he said. "Never seen anything like it. It made me want to support your pageant. You're the kind of community enterprise that Build Right likes to back."

"Wonderful," Bridget said. "What did you have in mind, Dave?"

He shrugged. "I'm open to suggestions. But this park leaves a lot to be desired. How about we bring in landscapers and turn it into a community dog hub?"

"Perfect." Bridget brightened. "I'd love to hold the pageant here and make the refurbishment a community event."

Mike's hands were waving like a referee's. He held a finger to his lips, then slashed across his throat and finally put both arms down as if calling a bad play. Bridget didn't need a translator to know it all led to "shut up."

"Great idea, Dave," Mike said at last. "Let's run that by Council. They might have other ideas."

"Of course," Dave said. "Whatever Mayor Bradshaw thinks is best."

Throwing a glare at Mike, Bridget stalked off to the ring, with Duff in pursuit. "Be nice, Bridget, be nice."

"I can't believe it. Mike used to be on my team."

"You don't pay his mortgage, Bee. The City does that."

Too angry to say more, Bridget gave Cori the sign to start the next training round. One of the contestants struggled to handle the Lab cross that had performed so beautifully for Trixie and Jonah. He jerked the leash around until the dog was thoroughly confused. Bridget got more and more agitated watching the dog stare up at the man, so eager to please and failing. Finally, the man gave the dog a little backwards kick to get its attention. Bridget recognized the move from a popular trainer, but that didn't stop her from hopping right into the ring.

"Did you kick that dog?" she demanded.

The man backed away from her. "It wasn't a kick, just a tap. He wasn't listening."

"Well, you listen to me: never kick a dog. Never." She held out her hand and he surrendered the leash. "You're disqualified. Goodbye."

Nika swept the man away before anything more could be said, and Duff pulled Bridget back out of the ring. "I said be nice, not aggressive."

"He kicked the dog, Duff. I'm not going to just stand by and let that happen. What kind of message would that send?"

"You don't have to stand by. You handle it quietly and tactfully. As if someone sent an order of food back and you still wanted to be tipped."

"This was a dog, not a hamburger."

"The dog wasn't harmed, but now a lot of people saw you lose your temper, Bee." Duff craned around. "I can only hope Dave from Build Right didn't see that. Now, fix your hair. You look like Medusa."

The breeze had picked up and Bridget ran her hands

through her loose curls and secured her ponytail again. "It doesn't matter how my hair looks. Can we focus on what's important?"

Duff turned to face Bridget and for once there was no trace of a smile on her lips. "That is what I'm trying to tell you, Bee. It *does* matter how your hair looks. In fact, your hair has never been more important and the future of the pageant may depend upon it."

Bridget stared, as if Duff had lost her mind. "That is ridiculous."

"Tell it to the stylist I'm bringing to your house tomorrow. My friend, you are about to get a makeover worthy of what you do to your rescue dogs."

"Won't happen." Bridget said. "Nope and never."

"Oh, it will. I'm your best friend, and I won't see you let everything you've worked so hard for fall into ruins because you refuse to adapt. It's survival of the fittest. And let me tell you this, Bridget: the fittest have great hair."

CHAPTER TWELVE

"Ouch, stop. Please. I'm begging you." Bridget swatted Duff's hand again and again as it zoomed in toward her face.

"It'll only hurt if you keep moving," Duff said. "Maisie?"

Maisie stepped forward and grabbed Bridget's head as if she were a prize poodle. "I wish I had my grooming noose."

Cori laughed from her perch on the counter. Bridget was sitting at the kitchen table while Duff spearheaded a makeover. She hadn't been able to line up a stylist on such short notice, so the mafia had done the heavy lifting themselves. Maisie had used her grooming shears to give Bridget's hair a surprisingly nice cut, and then straightened it with a high-powered dog dryer. Nika and Duff had buffed, plucked and dabbed using a huge palette of makeup. All that remained was curling the lashes, and Duff had already given Bridget's eyelid an accidental pinch.

"Ow! I can't. Leave it, Duff."

"I'm not leaving anything. Perfect lashes are like window treatments. It makes a house look done."

Bridget crossed her arms and turned her head. "Fine. Then I will be late for the wedding?"

"Late isn't an option," Duff said. "Girls?"

Nika and Maisie joined forces to subdue Bridget like a feral cat and subject her to forcible petting.

Running her fingers through Bridget's hair, Nika said, "I had no idea how shiny your hair was under that wave, Bee. It's gorgeous."

"Gorgeous," Maisie echoed. "You look like Beau."

"Excuse me?" Duff reared back. "Bridget most certainly does not look like a dog."

Maisie was taken aback. "I just meant their coats are similar. I mean, their hair."

Duff shot a scowl at her, but Bridget laughed. "It's a compliment. I'm flattered."

"Living room," Duff said, tipping the chair to make Bridget stand. "We have ten minutes to get you dressed."

The couch was heaped high with borrowed finery. Everyone except Cori had brought dresses for Bridget to try on. She hadn't been to a wedding or any other formal event in years, and her only 'little black dress' had been dubbed dated by Duff.

Bridget stopped resisting and let herself be dressed and undressed like a doll. Duff, Maisie and Nika conferred on each outfit, and took photos to compare notes. There was a lot of squealing and sighing, punctuated with occasional huffs of disgust from Cori, who'd sprawled across an oversized armchair.

Finally, the team settled on a fuchsia silk dress from Duff, strappy stilettos a half size too large from Nika, and a bag and coat from Maisie.

"You look stunning," Duff said. "If I do say so myself."

She snapped a photo and waved her phone under Bridget's nose.

"I don't even know that person," Bridget said. "She looks too precious to get her hands dirty."

"The hands..." Duff sighed. Bridget's short nails were freshly polished, but nothing could be done about the callouses. "I did the best I could."

Bridget pushed the phone away. "The mayor had better be at this gig, that's all I'm saying."

"He'll be there," Duff said. "Lindsay is the daughter of his golfing buddy. The old boys come out for weddings."

Straightening in the armchair, Cori said, "Let me get this straight: Bee goes to the wedding and seduces the mayor in the receiving line?"

"Receiving lines are so yesterday," Duff said. "And no seduction is required. Or permitted, actually."

"As if." Bridget shuddered. "I'd invite the bank to foreclose and live under the Monroe Street Bridge before I let that happen."

"Trolls have pride," Cori said.

"Exactly." Bridget hobbled to the door. "Trolls don't need to worry about falling off their heels and humiliating themselves."

"The plan, in case there's any doubt," Duff continued, "is for Bridget to bask in the bride and groom's gratitude for matching them at the pageant two years ago. The mayor, who was previously inclined to dismiss Bee, will be forced to acknowledge her talent."

"And her cleavage," Cori added.

"That's not mandatory," Duff said. "I have a scarf that works perfectly with that dress."

Bridget eyed herself in the mirror in the front hall. "Scarves are for sissies. Go big or stay home."

Nika and Maisie laughed and even Duff smiled.

"You really couldn't find any other way to impress the mayor?" Cori asked.

Turning, Bridget shrugged. "I was going to the wedding anyway. Lindsay asked me to wrangle Bruno up the aisle. He's the Dog of Honor. Or Best Dog. Or something."

Duff walked over and straightened the hem of the dress. "Which is great because the mayor can't miss you. Afterwards, you wait till he's had a glass or two and make your move. Stick to the script. And for heaven's sake, don't get tipsy yourself."

Bridget dangled the car keys. "I'm driving anyway."

"You are not arriving in that green van, Cinderella. You'll get dog hair all over my dress. I'll take you and pick you up in my coach."

"I assume you've got an earpiece on her so that you can talk her through every conversation?" Cori asked.

"Wish I'd thought of that." Duff looked like she meant it.

"I promise you, I will not blow this, Duff. The hardest part is going to be operating these shoes."

"Small steps. Make like a geisha," Nika said. "Don't risk a sprain so close to the pageant."

"True. So, no dancing," Duff said.

Bridget rolled her eyes. "Am I allowed to eat dinner? Lions need their strength to hunt."

"Yes, of course. Just check your teeth afterwards, and don't get pulled into too much small talk. Right after dessert, you make your move. Then you text for extraction. Got it?"

"Got it," Bridget said, slipping her arms into the coat Nika held out. "Piece of wedding cake."

BRUNO, a Boston terrier mix, turned into a whirling dervish when Bridget hobbled up the stairs of Dorset Hills Baptist, one of the oldest and prettiest churches in the city. The dog's tail lashed like a whip, but he didn't jump, he didn't mouth, and he didn't bark.

"He's still rock solid," Bridget told Lindsay, smiling as she joined the bridal party in the vestibule. "You've done well with him."

Under the sweep of veil, the bride's smile faded. "Oh, Bridget, I think we've made a terrible mistake. We agreed to take in Adam's sister's dog, Peaches, and Bruno's been miserable."

"How long has it been?"

"Two months. Adam won't hear a bad word about Peaches. Even though she's torn up the couch, and pees everywhere when we're at work."

"Separation anxiety." Bridget motioned for the three bridesmaids to adjust their position and then bent to rearrange Lindsay's train. When she straightened, she noticed the wedding planner's frown, and backed off quickly. Managing a pack was Bridget's default position. "Dogs need time to adjust when they've been rehomed. Cori and I will come visit after your honeymoon."

"Thank you." Lindsay leaned over to hug Bridget. "I didn't recognize you when you came in."

Bridget smirked. "That bad?"

"That good." She made as if to toss the bouquet. "I'll send this your way, later."

"I'll make sure my hands are full," Bridget said, grabbing Bruno's leash with both hands. "Don't waste that magic on me."

The bridal party moved to the entrance of the church, and one by one the bridesmaids sailed up the aisle. The wedding planner gave Bridget a little shove from behind and she moved forward with Bruno. "Eyes up. Chest forward," she told Bridget.

Bridget fought a giggle, realizing she'd practically become a show dog. She did as she was told, focussing on the pulpit, and pacing deliberately up the aisle. Bruno never missed a beat, and neither did she. Not even when she glanced sideways at the second pew and saw Mayor Bradshaw. Not even when she saw another familiar face in the same pew: Sullivan Shaw.

Taking a deep breath, she fell into position in front of the minister. Bruno sat like a statue through the ceremony and all the way back down the aisle. When they reached the church foyer, however, he began shivering uncontrollably. There was a sudden growl and a blur of gold. Bruno ended up on his back and pinned by a dog that looked like an over-sized cocker spaniel. A fanged Muppet. Peaches, she presumed. The crowd reared back and a few ladies screamed, which only spurred Peaches to turn up the volume and mouth Bruno's throat. He let out a screech.

Dropping his leash, Bridget bent and grabbed Peaches by the hind legs. Then she backed away, as if pulling a wheelbarrow. Peaches tried to turn but couldn't do much operating on only her front paws. Towing the dog into the church, Bridget dropped her legs and grabbed her leash all in one fluid movement. Then she gave a quick leash correction, and said, "Sit, Peaches. Watch me."

Miraculously, Peaches did as she was told. Then Bridget walked the dog up and down the aisle a couple of times until her tail was up, and her demeanor relaxed.

The groom stood in the doorway, wringing Bruno's

leash with both hands. "I'm sorry, Bridget. I didn't think she actually meant it."

"She didn't," Bridget said. "If she had, there'd be blood on Bruno's tuxedo."

"I shouldn't have brought her today. I just didn't want her to feel left out."

"Oh, Adam." Bridget shook her head. "They're not kids, but this will be good training if you plan on having any. Peaches is going to need strong leadership from you."

"Lindsay's crying," he said. "What do I tell her?"

She smiled. "Tell her you've taken care of everything— by letting me take care of everything. There won't be any canine casualties on my watch."

DUFF HAD BEEN wrong about the receiving line. Bridget stood with the wedding party for what seemed like hours in the foyer of the Larkson Grand Hotel. The boutique hotel was too small to be truly grand, but it had been renovated nicely in recent years. The whole area by the Larkson Marsh had been getting a facelift. Bridget had mixed feelings about that, but there was no question that the hotel had become the perfect wedding venue. Its many tall antique mirrors made the place look bigger, and reflected the beautiful orange, red and yellow bouquets. They'd worked the Thanksgiving angle beautifully.

By the time Mayor Bradshaw reached her in line, Peaches had settled down and become as sweet as her name implied.

"You handled that incident very well, young lady," the mayor said, flashing Bridget the movie star smile that had won him the women's vote. "I guess you've owned dogs before."

"Well, yes." Bridget eyed him dubiously. Was it possible he didn't recognize her? "That's why the Thanksgiving Rescue Pageant has been such a success, sir."

He blinked twice, just enough to give himself away. "Of course. Birdie, isn't it?"

"Bridget." She transferred the two leashes to her left hand so she could offer him her right, calibrating her grip carefully. Duff had made her practice, saying her usual handshake brought people to their knees. "Nice to see you again, Mayor."

He appraised her, and not in a salacious way. "You do look... different, Bridget."

"It's a wedding, sir. Not the beach. Or the hills." She gave him a sly smile. "I'm versatile."

"And still able to break up a dog fight without getting a hair out of place. Impressive." He beckoned a couple of men she guessed were golf club cronies. "This is Bridget. She organizes our Thanksgiving dog pageant. Bridget, these are my oldest friends, Roger and Neil."

"Gentlemen." The handshake came easily to Bridget this time. "My pageant brings people and rescue dogs together. And sometimes... just people. I'm not sure if you're aware, Mayor, but I matched the bride and groom."

She normally shied away from such claims, but Duff had predicted the mayor would respond positively.

"A matchmaker in Dorset Hills?" he said. "Fascinating."

"Every town needs one, sir. Especially a romantic place like Dog Town."

"My niece met a young man through your event," Roger said. "They're besotted with each other."

"Wonderful," Bridget said. "I'm eager to see what this

year will bring. Mind you, I do worry about holding the pageant in the hills. It can be slippery and unsafe at this time of year."

"She's got a point, Bill," Roger said. "My wife loves that event, and I wouldn't want her going up to the hills right now."

"Attendance might drop, and that would be a shame. I'm afraid we'd lose the media, too," Bridget said.

"I believe the beach was an option," the mayor said. "It's safe and it's central."

Bridget kept working her smile. "Oh, sir. Safe doesn't need to mean boring, does it? I have other ideas. It's not too late."

He rolled his eyes at his cronies. "Shoot."

"Well, I was thinking—"

"Bridget? Bridget!" The wedding planner bustled over. "Photos!"

The mayor smiled as Bridget resisted. "The show must go on, Birdie. We'll talk later."

After the photos were done, the mayor had been surrounded by an impenetrable crowd. Bridget took the opportunity to get the dogs outside. The courtyard behind the hotel was gorgeous in summer and she often met friends there for a drink. The bugs could be bad, but she loved hearing the frogs sing in the marsh.

By now, the frogs would be settling in to hibernate. Winter was sending threats on a stiff breeze.

The multicolored plastic lanterns glowed on the patio as the sun set and she went towards them, stumbling on the uneven flagstones. It was nice to have a reprieve from the crowd inside.

"Hey, Bridget."

She turned, startled. A couple was standing in the

shadow of the hotel. Peaches moved to the end of her leash and gave an imposing growl for a spaniel mix.

"Another savage," the man said. "Never a dull moment for you."

Sullivan Shaw, with his gazelle, Grace. She'd had the sense to put a coat on over her dress, unlike Bridget.

"It feels like a circus sometimes," Bridget said. "Sorry for disturbing you."

She turned too quickly and tripped over the leashes. Sullivan reached out to steady her. His hand felt warm on her cool skin—so warm that she moved away quickly. Her skin had no business tingling like that for Sullivan Shaw.

"I love your dress," Grace said. "So pretty."

"Pretty uncomfortable, actually." She crossed her arms, wishing she'd brought Duff's scarf after all. "At least for a tomboy like me. I used to come down here as a kid and catch tadpoles in the marsh."

Grace shuddered, but Sullivan laughed. "Kept them in a jar till they sprouted legs?"

"Yep. Coolest thing ever. Then I brought them back and set them free." Bridget laughed a little. "Sometimes I still come down to hear the frogs singing. I wonder how many generations have passed."

"You must be sad about the swamp then," Grace said.

"That they expanded the hotel? Yeah, I was."

"That they're draining the rest of it." Grace jerked back a bit, as if Sullivan had tried to silence her.

"What do you mean?" Bridget's grip on the leashes tightened and Peaches growled again.

"They're developing it. Putting up a low-rise and some shops. Sullivan can tell you more. He's part of the team."

"This isn't the time, Grace," Sullivan muttered.

The fury that started in the pit of Bridget's stomach chased away the chill. "You're destroying the marsh?"

"Not all of it." He sounded both sheepish and defiant. "There will be a park. Kids can still come down and catch tadpoles."

"I... I don't know what to say." Bridget's voice was tight and high. The only time of her childhood that she remembered with much fondness was about to crumble under the weight of Dorset Hills' progress. "I hate—" She stopped herself. She wanted to say *people like you*, but she knew Sullivan wasn't the cause of the development. Dorset Hills was growing in leaps and bounds. "I hate hearing things like that," she finished at last.

Sullivan buttoned his suit jacket. "I know it's hard to see things change in Dorset Hills. But the work will be done responsibly."

"Yes, of course." Bridget's voice was faint. "Excuse me... I need to walk the dogs."

She left them on the patio. It was past dusk now, and she picked her way carefully over the grass.

"Stay away from the bank," Sullivan called after her. "It's wet and muddy."

"For now," she called back. "Soon we'll be able to shop here."

If he answered, it was drowned in the babbling of the water as it came downstream before dispersing into the marsh. There was a fish ladder about half a mile upstream. Lake Longmuir wasn't exactly a thriving ecosystem, but it did foster a few salmon that came back to spawn. Where would they go now?

There was a loud splash in the water. A muskrat, she guessed, or an otter. Peaches leapt forward and yanked the leash out of Bridget's hand. Then there was a louder splash as the dog went off the bank and into the water. "Peaches! Peaches, come!"

Peaches wasn't coming. She was sloshing around in the darkness.

"Water dogs," Bridget said, cursing. "Peaches, come out of there."

The splashing came from higher upstream now. Peaches was enjoying her swim. Following the noise, Bridget walked along the bank. Bruno whimpered, and she wished she had Beau with her, instead. He'd collect Peaches and put her properly in her place. The dog would come out eventually, but in the meantime, Bridget was freezing in her skimpy dress.

"Let's try reverse psychology, Bruno," she said, turning, and hobbling in the opposite direction. It always worked with her own dogs, but where there was no bond there was no guarantee. However, Peaches turned out to be as smart as Bridget predicted. The splashing followed them downstream. Bridget remembered the geography well. Another sixty yards and the stream would start to dwindle. There was a small sandy stretch of shoreline where she could likely lure and leash Peaches.

Slowly and carefully, she edged along the bank. Just another few yards now, and Peaches was catching up.

Suddenly, there was a yelp, and thrashing in the water. "Peaches!" This time Bridget yelled and came close to the edge. The soft clay gave way and she plunged down the bank to land on her hands and knees in shallow water. "Ow, ow." The stones had cut her hands and knees, and her ankles twisted off the heels, but otherwise, she was okay. "Peaches!" And then, "Bruno, stay!" Luckily, she'd dropped the leash as she fell.

The splashing got nearer, and then, bam! The dog leapt

on Bridget and knocked her right over into the water. Thrashing, she managed to grab Peaches' leash. Holding it in her left hand, she pulled off her shoes and threw them up on the bank.

Floundering, she tackled the bank but slid down twice. Fear for Bruno kept her focussed. Finally, a light appeared over the side. Standing on the bank was Sullivan, with Bruno by his side. "Bridget, are you okay?"

"Take Peaches," she said, offering the leash up to him. He knelt and took it.

"Wait there." He disappeared for a moment, and then the light bobbed back. Bruno started howling.

Peeling off his suit jacket, Sullivan went down on one knee again and held his hand out to Bridget. She grasped his fingers tightly, and he pulled. The slime on her hand cost her his grip. He leaned forward to catch her as she slid back, and then he lost his balance too. Down the bank he came. The flashlight tumbled over and over in the water. Cursing, Sullivan clambered to his feet, and went after the light. It flickered, but stayed lit. Just as he grabbed it, the silty bottom gave way and tipped him into a deeper pool of water. He sat up, wet to his chin, unleashing a blue streak.

Bridget wanted to laugh, but her lips had frozen.

Scrambling out of the sinkhole, Sullivan shone the light on Bridget and pulled her up. "You're bleeding," he said.

"I'm fine." Bridget looked down and saw that Duff's pink dress was covered in sludge so heavy that it had pulled the already-low neckline even lower. Most of her wet bra was exposed and it was transparent. She yanked up the dress and crossed her arms over her chest.

"You're going to need those."

She glanced up and found Sullivan looking at her folded arms, grinning. A flush started somewhere down near her frozen feet and cascaded up to her face. She had never felt less appealing, but he seemed to like what he saw.

"Never mind," she said. "Where's Grace?"

"Inside. Waiting to call the cavalry if needed."

"And the dogs are safe?"

"Just unhappy about being tied to a tree." He turned to the bank and sized things up. "It's going to be a mud bath."

"We could walk down to the shallows."

"Too slippery and rocky for bare feet. Let's just do this."

Maneuvering Bridget in front of him, he lifted her as high as he could, and when she found a shrub to grab, moved his hands under her butt and kept shoving until she tipped over the top. Once she was on her feet, he threw the light to her and clawed his way up himself. Looking down at his clinging, filthy white shirt and slimy pants, he shook his head. "You had to relive your tadpole memories tonight? At a wedding?"

"Didn't work out like I planned," she said, picking her way across the lawn toward the wailing dogs. "I'm sorry, Sullivan. And thank you."

She tried to unhook the dogs' leashes but her fingers were too cold. He bent and released them for her. Watching her shake in great wracking spasms, he tossed her his jacket. "Give me the dogs. I'll take them inside and then drive you home."

"You can't go in there like that," she said.

"Well, you certainly can't go in there like that." He glanced down at her bra again, and this time his grin lit up the darkness. "Although the mayor might pay more attention."

"Doubt it." She slipped into the jacket and clutched it closed. "He likes a polished presentation."

Sullivan unbuttoned his mucky shirt and peeled it off.

Bridget stared at his bare chest, mesmerized. It was obvious that destroying and rebuilding was good for his physique.

He caught her looking and kept grinning. She expected him to tease her, but he just said, "Let's get you warmed up."

Grace came outside carrying Sullivan's coat. She gasped when she saw them, but said nothing. Sullivan declined the coat and simply walked inside bare-chested. Grace followed, without even glancing over her shoulder.

Bridget waited until the door closed behind them. Then she ran.

CHAPTER THIRTEEN

"You just hopped in a cab?" Duff's eyebrows seemed to be stuck in the raised positioned as she steered her SUV through the heavy traffic downtown. Normally, Bridget insisted on driving but she was stiff and sore from her adventure the night before.

"It was more like a slither, actually," Bridget said. "Then I crouched in the footwell like a fugitive. Good thing it was only a ten-minute drive."

Duff pumped the gas and then the brake. "You should have called me, Bee."

"No phone, remember?" She braced herself on the dashboard and winced. Her palms were still raw. "I just wanted to get home. Took me an hour in the bath to thaw out."

"I'll bet. Stupid Peaches."

"I went back to the hotel this morning to collect my stuff. Nika's shoes are ruined and your dress is on life support at the dry cleaners. They're making no promises."

"I don't care about the dress. I'm just glad you're okay."

Bridget held out her palms. "The wounds to my pride go far deeper."

"I hate to ask about the mayor, but..."

"That's one reason I bolted. I didn't want to undo the progress I'd made."

"Okay, good. I mean, it wasn't good, obviously. But it was gallant of Sullivan."

Bridget gave a dismissive wave. "He's still a slimy developer. Outside now, as well as in."

"Cut him a break. He has different priorities, that's all."

"Yeah, wrecking everything good in this town."

Duff's hand hovered over the horn at an intersection. Several people sauntered across with their dogs even after the light had turned red. "Come on, move it," she said.

"Don't honk. You know what they say..."

"Scare the dog, beware the owner." Duff snorted. "Dog people think they can flout every traffic light. Honestly."

"Your road rage fascinates me." It was the reason Bridget usually drove despite Duff's complaints about dog hair in the van. "You're so smooth everywhere else it has to bubble up somewhere, I guess."

Duff shook her finger at an old lady and her poodle, and then shook it at Bridget as well. "Never mind."

"That's exactly what I told Sullivan when he ogled my boobs in the creek last night."

Duff braked hard for a red light. "He ogled?"

"And smirked."

A grin swept across Duff's face. "Really! And where was Grace during his facial gymnastics?"

"Avoiding the swamp and the dogs. Smart lady."

A loud honk made them both jump. The light had turned green and they hadn't moved forward. Duff exchanged her index finger for her middle one as she pounded the gas.

"Cool your jets, will you?" Bridget said. "We've still got fifteen minutes."

"We're back-to-back with two house calls before meeting Mike at City Hall. We can't afford to be held up by idiots." Duff made a hard right followed by a hard left. Now they were driving parallel to Main Street on Lonsdale Avenue. The atmosphere in the car cleared as they flew. "So Sullivan wasn't put off by your stink?"

"Excuse me?"

"My friend, you still smell of marsh sludge—even after that hour-long bath."

"And a few showers on top." Bridget grinned. "Well, I bet he smells even worse. You should have seen him go down in that sinkhole. Good thing my lips had frozen, because I only laughed inside."

"You can laugh, but I think your frog man is going to turn into a prince."

"For Grace, and she's welcome to him." Bridget pumped an invisible brake. "Slow down, jeez. I want to live to see the pageant." The car circled some jaywalking teens, practically blowing their hoods back. "I feel kind of bad I never noticed before how pretty Grace is. She's got that sexy librarian vibe. Frogman's bringing that out in her."

"Meh. She'd blow away in a stiff breeze. Men like women they can mud wrestle."

"Says the woman whose hair is always perfect."

"In public, my friend. In private, it's a whole different cage match."

Two phones buzzed simultaneously, in Duff's lap and Bridget's.

"Uh-oh," Bridget said. "Must be a 911." Grabbing her

phone, she confirmed it. "Turn right at the next intersection, Duff."

"Bee, we can't." Duff's voice was pleading.

"It's a rescue emergency. We have no choice."

Sighing, Duff turned and drove at breakneck speed toward the outskirts of town. "This is really bad timing."

"There's no good time for a rescue 911. If a dog's in desperate need, house calls can wait."

"But the debut is on Saturday and the pageant five days after that. Besides, urgent rescues are so risky, Bee. Any negative press would be deadly right now." Bridget didn't respond, so Duff continued. "Let the girls handle this one. If you want to make it through Thanksgiving without the wheels falling off, you're going to have to delegate more."

"Nika and Maisie don't have enough experience," Bridget said. "And Cori's a wild card."

"Less so, lately. You used to be a wild card too."

"Guess we're all learning from you to try diplomacy before combat." Bridget drummed her fingers on the dash. "How about I keep the meeting with Mike, and you work with the girls on the rescue to make sure it goes well?"

"Deal. I have a hat and sneakers in the hatch." The only time Duff lowered herself to flats was a 911, where speed and agility might mean the difference between saving a dog and getting arrested.

Duff steered off the main artery into Holmburg, a suburb that got little profile in Dorset Hills. The houses were packed together, many of them dilapidated.

Taking an old gravel road, they drove toward the trail head. They were on the south side of the range of hills, fifteen miles from the main trails and Clifford's Crest. Council had vowed years ago to connect the entire trail system, but it hadn't happened yet. When the local citizens complained, the new mayor had renewed his commitment by delivering one of the original bronze dog sculptures.

That was why a huge chow-chow sat at the start of the rough trail, surrounded by scrubby bush. They could just see the tips of his ears as they pulled into the gravel parking lot. Cori's truck and Nika's car were parked at the far end.

"Why a chow-chow, anyway?" Duff asked, sending up a cloud of dust as she sped towards Cori's truck. "Out here, a hound or a setter would make more sense."

"You're expecting the City to make sense?" Bridget said. "Someone must have backed out of their sponsorship. I heard these statues go for twenty grand. Imagine what that money could do for services for dogs. People like us wouldn't have to do the dirty work."

They got out of the car and crunched over the gravel to the start of the trail. Cori, Nika and Maisie were perched along the platform at the chow-chow's feet. The dog was majestic, with a gorgeous ruff. His soft eyes looked out over the valley below—or they would if the brush were cleared. Bridget felt bad for the chow, stuck out here all alone. The City hadn't included him on maps or the bus tour to discourage people from using unmaintained trails. He was orphaned, like the dogs they saved.

Cori got up and motioned for Bridget to take her place. "Sit down, Bee. I have some bad news. Geronimo, the bichon-corgi cross you placed, needs to be extracted."

"Geronimo?" Bridget jumped to her feet immediately. "How can that be? Tina Munro was the perfect owner."

"Until she hooked up with a loser," Cori said. "And then left him and Geronimo. One of their neighbors is part of the rescue network. She says the dog is a mess—left outside day and night."

Tears sprang to Bridget's eyes. "Geronimo's a lapdog. He's not built for outdoor kenneling."

"There's no kennel. Just a cardboard box, apparently. My informant is worried about how the dog will fare when it gets colder. He howls all the time as it is."

Nika pulled tissues out of her bag and passed them around. Everyone except Cori was crying. Maisie's were angry tears, and she scraped them away with her sleeve. "He's the sweetest dog I ever groomed. Let's get him out of there today."

"The loser boyfriend apparently leaves for work at three," Cori said. "If we wait till sundown, we won't be seen."

Bridget paced back and forth. "Why didn't Tina just give him back? My contract says the dog must be returned if the owner's circumstances change."

"From what I hear, she left in a hurry a couple of weeks ago after a huge fight," Cori said. "But my contact expected Tina to come back for the dog so she didn't call right away. Today she saw an eagle circling the yard, and Geronimo's small enough to be in trouble."

Bridget kicked a shrub, got her boot tangled, and nearly fell. "Let's deploy."

"Wait, Bee." Duff's voice was calm. "Think this through."

"There's nothing to think about." Bridget paced again. "One of my dogs is in danger."

Duff stepped in front of her. "Diplomacy over combat, remember? If we steal the dog, it might make the news, and we don't want press like that before the pageant. Maybe it's better to go in and convince the guy it's in his best interest to return the dog."

"I don't think I could face him." Bridget stepped around Duff. "Let's just get in and get out."

"Agreed," Cori said. Nika and Maisie echoed the word.

Duff held firm. "I know it's your right to reclaim the dog, but even in these circumstances, it's going to cause talk. People will say you chose the wrong winner in Tina. This is the first time one of your matches has ever gone wrong, Bridget. It could make people doubt the whole process. Better to keep it quiet, if we can. Just ask him nicely for the dog back."

Cori turned on Duff. "She doesn't need to be nice to someone abusing a dog—a dog we all cared for and trained."

"Look at the subtleties, Cori. Bridget contracted with the girlfriend. It should be easy enough to get him to surrender Geronimo. He might even be grateful to be rid of him. Then we can look after the dog and keep it all quiet."

Bridget rubbed her forehead with both hands. "There's a limit to how fake I can be."

"Just think strategically," Duff pressed.

"But what if he doesn't hand over the dog? Then it will get even uglier than if we just extracted Geronimo in the first place."

"I'm sure you can talk him into it."

"*You* can talk him into it while I sit on my hands to keep from strangling him," Bridget said.

"Possibly, but it probably makes more sense for me to go meet with Mike at City Hall. We can't afford to cancel that."

Bridget walked over to the bronze chow-chow and ran her hands over his cold metal flank. Then she rested her hot forehead against him. "Poor little Geronimo. I think I'm going to be sick."

Cori looked up from her phone. "If we're going to talk to

this guy, we've got about an hour before he leaves for work. Deploy?"

"Deploy," Bridget said.

DANIEL QUINTO MOVED out of the doorway to allow them to pass and then gestured to the living room. Bridget, Cori and Nika all sat on the loveseat. It was a tight fit.

Bridget got up again. Daniel was about her height and she wanted to meet him eye to eye.

"Thanks for seeing us, Daniel. As I said, we're just doing quick check-ins on our past pageant winners before Thanksgiving. I can't wait to see Geronimo. He was one of my favorites."

Daniel wasn't tall, but he was broad. His face would be handsome if not for small, cold eyes. Why hadn't Tina noticed the eyes? When Bridget interviewed her two years ago, Tina was engaged to a great guy. Daniel must have been the rebound mistake.

"You're better to come back when Tina's here," he said. "The dog's fine but he never really took to me. I don't think much of froufrou dogs."

"Most men like big dogs," Bridget said, forcing up the corners of her lips. "Is he outside? I'll pop out and see him."

She took a step toward the kitchen, and Daniel swiftly blocked her path. "Come back another day."

A chill went down Bridget's spine. It might be three against one, but she suspected Daniel would be a match for all of them. "We're here now. I have 20 more dogs to visit in just over a week."

He shrugged. "Not my problem."

"Well, Tina would want me to see Geronimo, I'm sure."

"You don't know Tina as well as you think you do. She let that dog get away with murder. He barks all the time and bit me a few times."

"That's awful! It sounds like I messed up his training." Bridget turned away from Cori. "I had better take Geronimo back for a while to correct these things."

Daniel crossed his arms. "No."

Bridget gave a hard, bright smile. "It's in my contract. I'm obligated to rehabilitate the dog if it's not meeting expectations."

"Your contract is with Tina. And this little brat apparently meets *her* expectations. So the dog stays until she gets back to deal with him."

Bridget's breaths came short and fast. She forced herself to slow down, for the good of the dog. "Where is she, anyway?"

"Ask her."

"Sure. Cori, can you text Tina now? We'll just wait."

Daniel raised his shoulders a little in a shrug. "You'll be waiting awhile."

"That's okay. There's nothing more important to me than the welfare of my dogs." Bridget wedged herself between Cori and Nika. "Tell us about yourself, Daniel."

He lowered himself slowly into an armchair and shook his head.

"Not much for small talk, I guess?"

"Not with dog crazies," he said. "You guys have wrecked this town for normal people like me."

Cori's left hand balled into a fist, but she kept her eyes on her phone. They'd agreed Bridget would do all the talking, and miraculously, she'd kept her word.

"I hear you," Bridget said. "Dorset Hills is a bit much, isn't it?"

"I gotta get out of this town," he said. "Geronimo will like it better down south where the sun shines."

"Wouldn't we all?" Bridget's tinkly laugh sounded like it belonged to someone else.

Cori's phone buzzed and she jumped to her feet. "We'll need to postpone, Bridget. Time for your meeting at City Hall."

Daniel didn't move so much as an eyebrow. "Let yourselves out, ladies."

"We will," Bridget said. "Nice to meet you, Daniel. I'll be back when I hear from Tina, okay?"

"Can't wait," he said.

By the time they reached Cori's truck, Daniel was in the doorway, watching.

Cori backed out of the driveway and drove off slowly. "Times like this, I wish we were mafia for real," she said.

"Brains over bloodshed," Bridget said, heaving a sigh as she leaned back in her seat.

CHAPTER FOURTEEN

Duff stood on a portable stage set up in Seaton Dog Park, quietly issuing directions to a dozen volunteers. It was another remarkably beautiful Saturday for November. Duff couldn't take credit for that, but what she had pulled off so far was nothing short of amazing. By this point, a week and a half before Thanksgiving, Bridget was usually overwhelmed and things started falling through the cracks. Nothing fell through the cracks on Duff's watch. She was a machine, gesturing here and there with a pencil. Nika rolled a red carpet down a ten-foot runway, as two men set up monitors so that the crowd could get a good look at the rescue dogs in their formal debut. Maisie was brushing and fluffing the dogs behind a hay bale barrier, and Cori was organizing the pageant's human contestants as they came into the park.

"What am I supposed to be doing?" Bridget asked. "Seems like I'm the only one without a job."

"Without you, no one would have a job," Duff said. "But since you asked... your job is to look good and play nice with others."

"Ugh." Bridget rolled her eyes. "Can't I just get my hands dirty?"

"Not before glad-handing the mayor."

"If he even shows up."

"Mike promised he'd be here. And I want you to turn on some serious charm with the mayor's cronies and any other local business representatives. Don't leave his side, and flirt if you have to, because sponsorships are down a bit this year."

"That's because of the venue. No one's big on the hills. I should have gone for the beach after all."

Duff looked around the dog park. "Honestly, Bee, your instincts were right. Seaton is the perfect venue for the pageant. We just need to convince the mayor of that today."

"It's too late to change the venue. Everyone knows it's at Clifford's Crest."

"Like it's ever hard to spread the word in Dog Town," Duff said. "Just whisper something and 500 people will know in an hour."

"True enough." Bridget started setting up folding chairs on the stage. "The problem is keeping things quiet."

"Which is why stealing Geronimo was insane." Duff's voice dropped to a low growl. "Someone's going to talk."

"It's not stealing when it's my dog." She gave Duff a defiant look. "I tried it your way, but when the charm offensive failed, I reclaimed him."

"Daniel called the police, Bee."

Luckily, by the time he got around to it, several neighbors had already called the cops and animal services to report seeing an eagle fly off with poor Geronimo. Falsely, of course. The little dog was far away from Dorset Hills and safe now.

"Hopefully the police will track down Tina and make

sure she's okay," Bridget said. "I can't believe she'd leave a dog with that guy. He's sinister."

Duff pointed her pen at Bridget. "Please try to stay out of trouble. You need to take this seriously."

Bridget snapped a chair open with such force that it came apart. "I *am* taking it seriously. I know what's at stake. But rescuing dogs will always come first to me." She took a few breaths, and then put the chair back together. "If I have to lose the house and move into your basement, I will."

"I don't have a basement, remember?"

"Right, so we'll sell my house at a profit and buy one together. Maybe that's what we should have done in the first place."

Duff smiled in spite of herself. "Call me old-fashioned, but I'd like to set up house with a guy. I haven't given up on love."

"I have." Bridget rested her hand on Beau's head. "I've got all I need right here."

"Look, Bee. People already talk about us enough without you joking that you're married to your dog."

"Not married. Just in a deeply fulfilling relationship with a male who only wants to please and never talks back."

"In other words, not a man. Look, just keep your weird to yourself when the mayor gets here." Duff appraised her friend. "You look great, by the way. Did you straighten your hair yourself?"

"Yep. Nearly passed out from the effort. As for the clothes, I actually feel pretty good." She did a pirouette. "I guess my transformation is complete."

"If you're stealing dogs, you're the old Bridget. Be the new Bridget."

"Lions take what they need, Duff."

Duff gave her a little shove. "I regret that analogy.

Now, I want you to be the eye of the storm. Let everyone else buzz around, while you stay calm and in your genius zone."

"Works for me." Bridget perched on a folding chair. "You're doing all the work and I'm sitting pretty. Genius, right?"

"Stay." Duff moved towards the stairs. "When the mayor arrives, you know what to do."

Bridget sighed, but she was actually happy taking orders from Duff. At first it had been hard to trust that anyone could do the work as well as she could. Now that she wasn't burdened with set design, promotion and myriad other details, however, she could do what she did best—focus on matching dogs and people. Apparently, all she had to do was remain the calm center. If only she'd ever *had* a calm center.

"Hey. I see you survived your tadpole expedition."

Sullivan was standing beside the stage, and for once he was without his sidekick. Bridget came to the side of the stage and jumped down lightly. He steadied her with one hand on the small of her back. It took her a second to realize she should move away. Even through her coat, his hand felt... nice. Calming.

"Sorry for taking off like that," she said, finally moving aside. "I just couldn't bear seeing the bride's face when the dogs came in."

"Or the bride's dress after Peaches jumped on her," Sullivan said. "What a mess."

"I paid for dry cleaning. I guess I should pay for yours, too. I'm assuming you stank as much as I did?"

"Almost," he said, and smiled. "Luckily the hotel staff found me a shower curtain to wrap myself in so I didn't get muck all over the car."

Bridget couldn't help grinning at the image. "Did you get a picture?"

"Like I'd show you." He grinned back. "Wish I'd taken one of you before you skulked off. Waste of a pretty dress."

Heat flared in Bridget's cheeks. "May it rest in peace. Couldn't be saved."

"What a shame," said Grace. She'd appeared out of nowhere, as she often did at the bistro. She took up less space than normal people.

"I hate dresses anyway," Bridget said. "At least, I used to."

"Something's changed?" Sullivan asked.

Bridget sighed. "Pretty much everything's changing."

She didn't mean anything in particular, but Sullivan's smile faded. "Sorry you had to hear about the marsh that way."

"Maybe Bridget doesn't mind so much now," Grace said. "The marsh is gross."

"It's beautiful to me," Bridget said. "I see value in things others throw away."

Sullivan pressed his lips together as if to bite off harsh words. When he spoke, his voice was pleasant. "I'm sure you'll find tadpoles there next spring, as always."

Keep it light, keep it fake, Bridget told herself. "Well, time marshes on, even in Dorset Hills." She backed a few steps away. "Guess I'd better marsh back to work."

"Wait." Sullivan shoved his hands into the pockets of his leather jacket. "Bridget, I'm not trying to stir up trouble, I promise you. But I wanted you to know that your dogs have been barking."

She stood very still. "What do you mean? All dogs bark sometimes."

"Not like this. They're—uh, I don't know—howling.

Like a—" He changed course. "I just thought you'd want to know."

"Like a *what*?" she pressed.

"Honestly? Like a pack of coyotes. All different sounds, like the craziest dog choir ever."

"That's ridiculous." Bridget stared at him. "I've been home every night. You've got the wrong dogs."

Sullivan looked away from her angry gaze. "I've heard it in daytime. But it is your dogs, I'm sure of that."

Bridget turned away. "I don't believe you. And I'm not going to get upset before this event. It's too important to me. Goodbye."

Pushing the discussion out of her mind, Bridget walked to the gate where a crowd had gathered. At the center of it was Mayor Bradshaw, along with Mike, a couple of young political aides, and a few men Bridget didn't recognize.

"There she is now, the Patron Saint of Dog Rescue," the mayor said, taking Bridget's hand in a firm grip. "You look lovely, hon."

"Thank you, Mayor. Nice of you to say so." Bridget noticed that it hardly hurt at all to be pleasant. Perhaps it would stick and she'd be fake year-round. "I'm so glad you could make it today. This is going to melt your heart."

"You're assuming I have one," he teased, guiding her toward the stage with a hand behind her elbow.

Along the way, others were sucked in by the mayor's gravitational pull, including Sullivan and Grace.

"Oh, sir, I know all about your poodle, Princess," Bridget said. "Any man who owns a dog has a big heart. Any man without one is suspect."

"I tend to agree with you there," the mayor said. He waved Mike and his retinue away as they walked. "Now, tell me about what's happening today."

Bridget stuck to the mayor like a burr for the next half hour, smiling, joking and mingling as if her career depended on it. Then she took him to the small VIP area Duff had cordoned off with velvet rope and sat beside him. Duff caught her eye from the stage and winked. This was all politics, Bridget supposed. And if flirting and cajoling would help save dogs in need in Dorset Hills, she was fine with that. Now that she was getting the hang of it, it felt like any other job.

"You've done a wonderful job capturing the spirit of the season," the mayor said, admiring the decorations Duff and Maisie had set up on the stage. Instead of the typical pumpkin patch hokeyness, they'd found very tall vases and filled them with even taller bundles of grasses tied with brown and gold ribbon. Other clear vases were filled with hundreds of the multicolored miniature gourds banned by City Council. Cori had already scared off kids with nefarious designs on them.

"I'm thankful for my artistic and talented friends," Bridget said. "The best is yet to come."

Duff picked up a microphone and got the show rolling. First, she introduced the 24 short-listed human contestants, who paraded in a row down the runway, pumping their arms, dancing and generally hamming it up. The crowd applauded and cheered, and the mayor joined in.

Then Duff called for silence and signaled to the tech volunteers. In the space of a week, volunteers had assembled a short video of each of the 12 rescue dogs. Bridget had recorded the voiceover, describing the conditions in which the dog had been found, and its long road of recovery. After each video played on big monitors, Niki walked the featured dog down the runway as strobe lights flashed. She had the dog sit, lie down, roll over, stand and give a play bow before walking back.

There was hardly a dry eye in the dog park, other than Bridget's and the mayor's.

"Well," he said, glancing around. "You certainly know how to play to your audience."

"Everyone loves a story where the underdog comes out on top, sir. Don't you agree?"

He gave Bridget an appraising look. "I think I underestimated you, Birdie."

"Really? How so?"

"If I'm honest, the pageant seemed dated and stale. You've shown me today you can take old faithful and give it a facelift."

Bridget smiled. "Makeovers are my speciality, you know."

He stood and smoothed his jacket and pants. "Tell me what you need to make my first Thanksgiving as mayor an event to remember."

Having rehearsed her pitch with Duff several times, Bridget launched into it seamlessly now. "Sir, I want to hold the event here. This is probably the worst dog park in the city, and we can make it the best in just a few hours. We'll resurface it, add some planters, and build an agility course, just for starters. I'd love to install a pond with a fountain."

"A pond sounds a little ambitious." He was smiling though. "And expensive to maintain."

"It's an investment, mayor. People come to places like this and hang out for hours. In Dorset Hills, the dog park might just be the most powerful meeting ground. By fostering community spirit you'll gain support for the changes you want to make."

"You're starting to think like a politician," the mayor said, leading her back to the entrance.

"Oh, sir, you flatter me," Bridget said.

They both laughed.

"All right, I'll find you some sponsors and drum up support for building supplies, refreshments, and whatever landscaping you can do in November. But I'm not promising a fountain."

"Wonderful. We'll put everyone to work on Thanksgiving, sir. Including you."

He chuckled. "No one likes a politician with dirty hands, Birdie."

"You can wash them in the fountain, sir. And please... call me Bridget."

Leaving with his entourage, the mayor gave a backwards wave. "Nothing wrong with Birdie."

CHAPTER FIFTEEN

The sun was low in the sky as Bridget drove home after a day of visiting sponsors with Duff and organizing the refurbishment of Seaton Park. The prospect of a hot shower and a cuddle with the dogs on the couch had never been more appealing. Still, she slowed to enjoy the drive along the twisting, hilly road. Plenty of leaves still clung to the trees, burning bright as the sun sank. Usually rain or high winds had claimed them by now. The sentinel oaks at the bottom of the driveway were almost bare, but their thick boughs seemed to reach out to welcome her home.

Home. This place had felt like home since the day of the viewing. And every day since, that feeling had grown.

Beau clearly agreed. He'd been standing in the passenger seat since they'd turned off the main road, his feathery tail fanning into her eyes.

Maybe that was why she didn't see the white van until she'd practically pulled up beside it. On the bright side, she hadn't run into it.

Officer Moller jumped down from his van when she slipped out of hers, leaving Beau inside. All she needed was for the dog to protect his turf against the Canine Corrections Department. As it was, he barked fiercely from the driver's seat.

"Good evening, ma'am," Officer Moller said.

"Hello, Dog Officer Moller," she replied. "What brings you here again?"

He cleared his throat in preparation. "There's been another complaint, ma'am."

"The number of my dogs hasn't changed, and it won't until Thanksgiving. At that point, I'll be left with only this one."

He looked at the car. The black dog whirling and hurling itself at the glass looked like some kind of specter, although the thuds were real enough. "One's probably enough."

"I'm in the business of many, though." She leaned against the car and crossed her arms, trying to block Beau's view. The dog hopped into the back to continue his assault on the glass.

Pulling out his phone, Officer Moller read from the rap sheet. "Ms. Linsmore, there have been complaints about disruptive barking at your residence."

Bridget's stomach sank. "Complaints? Plural?"

"On multiple occasions, yes. I can send the dates to you."

"By multiple people, or just one person, making multiple complaints?"

"I'm not at liberty to say, ma'am."

Again with the ma'am-ing. It felt like a tactic. But she was determined to put up a good defence. "How am I to address the so-called complaint when I don't know who's making it?"

"You're not, ma'am. We are. All you need to address is the barking."

"Alleged barking." She pushed herself off the car and walked towards him. "It's Sullivan Shaw's word against mine."

"I can't speak to the source or sources of complaint, ma'am. But I assure you, the noise has been verified by the CCD."

"Verified how?" She was right in front of him now, but he didn't step back, as she'd expected.

"With recordings on several occasions, ma'am."

"Recordings? It could be any dogs."

He pulled out his phone and pressed with his thumb until a loud cacophony began. Sullivan had been right. It was like an unholy coyote choir.

"That's not my dogs. I don't know what that is, but listen." She gestured toward the house. "They're all in there and they're not making a peep."

"It is your dogs. I recorded it myself yesterday afternoon. And the day before... *this*." He pressed again and more eerie barking ensued. The volume went up and up, although he wasn't adjusting it. She couldn't pick out any one voice in the crowd.

Suddenly a yodeling howl rose in the recording. It was immediately echoed by a yodel inside the house. Fritz.

"I don't understand." Bridget groaning, pressing fingertips into her temples to keep her head from exploding. "My dogs hardly ever bark, let alone howl. Only Beau barks. He's the lead dog."

He shrugged. "Maybe they howl when their lead dog's not here. I'm no expert on pack dynamics. All I can tell you is that this noise exceeds the allowable decibels for a residential neighborhood."

It would exceed the allowable decibels inside the gates of hell, Bridget thought. "It sounds like I'll need to have a talk with them, Officer."

"If you want to make it to the pageant, you'll need to do more than that, ma'am."

"More threats, Officer?"

"Well, that's the second complaint. Again, I'm authorized to remove the dogs."

Bridget took a deep breath, and then another, but the delay only prevented her from actually striking him. When she spoke, her voice was quiet, but ominous. "Over. My. Dead. Body."

Officer Moller blinked a few times and cleared his throat again. "That won't be necessary. Maybe you could have someone stay with them while you're out. Or use muzzles."

"Muzzles! Muzzles would traumatize them. This is a big week for the dogs and I can't afford to upset them."

He got back in the van, rolled down the window and hit play again. "Ma'am, like I said, I'm no expert on pack dynamics. But it sounds to me like your pack is traumatized already."

Bridget clung to the edge of his window. "Wait. I can't afford another complaint. One more and—"

"You'll ruin your chances for a kennel permit. I know. That's why I came twice to verify before proceeding."

"But Officer..."

"I don't like having to do this, ma'am. I'm a dog lover, too. This bothers me as much as it does you."

Bridget suddenly felt as small as a child looking up at him. "I very much doubt that, Officer. Unless you're about to cry right now."

He gunned it out of the driveway, shooting gravel back like tiny bullets.

"NO WHINING," Bridget said, holding her phone over her head as a flashlight.

Beau pushed behind her, making distressed peeps.

"I don't like having to do this, Beau. This bothers me as much as it does you."

He panted an anxious rebuttal. Beau had never liked adventures after dark, particularly in the bush when something might jump out at them.

"Sorry, I don't care. I'm not going over there alone. And this is probably preferable to being in the house with 12 coyotes."

Finally, after falling twice, Bridget emerged on Sullivan's driveway. She hadn't stopped to consider that he might not be home. Or that driving over made more sense. She'd left her driveway on the winds of rage and descended on his deflated. Now she was here, and his silver sports car was shining under the porch light. She might as well have a word with him. What that word would be, she'd didn't know. Hopefully she'd be as eloquent as she had been with the mayor yesterday. Dealing with asses was just another element of her job now.

She rapped the knocker once, easing Beau behind her. "Be nice. That's how we roll, buddy."

The porch light came on and Sullivan opened the door, looking disheveled and surprised. His dark hair was tousled and his face stubbly. He was the kind of guy who could practically grow a beard overnight. "Bridget. Hi."

"Why?" That was the only word that came to mind. "Why?"

He stepped out the door and let it close behind him. "The city needs more housing, that's why. But we're going to preserve a section of the marsh, I promise you. It's an important part of the Dorset Hills ecosystem."

"No." She waved her hand, but still couldn't spit out her real reason for coming.

"I know it's upsetting, and I feel bad about the tadpoles and frogs." He hopped on the cold porch, and then held up one bare foot against the opposite leg. "And the herons. And whatever else is in that stinking cesspool. Seriously, I do. But you can't let it upset you this much."

A few tears trickled down Bridget's cheeks, and she dashed them away with her sleeve. "Don't poke my butt," she said.

"Pardon me?" he said. "I'm not—"

"Not you, the dog. He's, er, nudging my butt."

"Oh. Well then." He smiled. "Can't blame a guy for that."

Some tiny muscles revived and tugged at the corners of Bridget's mouth. "Never mind."

"Come in." Sullivan stepped back. "And bring the dog, even though he hates my guts."

"He doesn't hate you."

Beau had to be pulled inside, and the hackles on his back rose as fast as his tail dropped.

Sullivan took another step back. "Obviously, he does. I have no idea why."

"He doesn't hate anyone else," Bridget said. "You should feel special."

Sullivan led her into the living room and motioned to a long, deep, chestnut leather couch—a man cave couch. The walls were paneled with cedar, and a massive fireplace sat full of logs waiting to be lit. Meanwhile, a football game played silently on an equally huge TV screen. Grace certainly hadn't made any inroads here. Her doll collection would run screaming.

"Dogs usually like me," Sullivan said, taking the armchair opposite and flinging his leg over the arm. "I guess Beau's the only one who knows about my missing heart."

"Pardon me?"

"You told the mayor yesterday that a man without a dog is a man without a heart. If I got that right."

"Close enough," she said. "If you called the city about my dogs' barking, you truly are heartless. These rescues are set to join amazing homes in a few days, but someone's putting their futures in jeopardy."

"I didn't call the city. I'm the one who warned you about the barking, remember?"

"I didn't believe you. And I heard nothing myself."

"It's happened a lot lately. But I didn't think you'd welcome a call about it."

"I may not have welcomed the news, but I'd have been grateful." She sighed. "At least, later. When my dogs weren't snatched out of my care."

Sullivan straightened up and leaned forward. "They took the dogs?"

"Not yet, but the dog cop reminded me he's within his rights to do so. One more complaint and I'm doomed. Some-one's got it in for me."

"Not me."

"If not you, then whom?"

"I'm not the only one with ears, Bridget. They could hear that wailing in Pemsville. And if you think I'm exag-gerating—"

"I heard a recording. Fritz's yodel was unmistakable."

"Ah, Fritz. He's quite a character." Sullivan smiled. "If I had a heart, that's the dog who'd prove it."

"You could have almost any dog," Bridget said. "Why didn't you go get a nice Lab after I turned you down?"

He smoothed the leather on the armrest. "Guess I figured you were right—that I wasn't ready for another dog. I had the perfect dog once, you know. Lightning probably doesn't strike twice."

"You didn't mention losing your perfect dog in your application. I'd remember that."

His eyes fixed on the TV screen. "I don't like to talk about it. Even after 10 years."

"Okay, but knowing that might have made a difference."

Probably not, though. Beau, who was sitting perfectly still beside her, had cast his vote clearly. And whatever he saw in Sullivan then, he saw now.

Still looking at the TV, Sullivan said, "Maybe it was for the best. I decided to make sure I was doing it for the right reasons, and not just because I was the new kid in town and lonely."

"It's not personal, Sullivan. These dogs are rescues. Every last one of them has a troubled past. I have to be careful to place them in the right homes, so they'll flourish. It doesn't mean you wouldn't raise a perfectly good dog from scratch."

"Right, I'm just not good enough for your dogs." He was teasing, but she could hear the hurt behind his words. He got up, turned to the fireplace, and started crumpling sheets of newspaper into balls.

"No one's good enough for my dogs," Bridget said, over the crumpling. "If I could keep them all, I would. But if the

CCD has its way, I'll only be able to keep four. That's why I need to figure out who's targeting me."

Sullivan bent to tuck balls of newspaper into the carefully arranged firewood. "Do you know the secret of a good fire, Bridget?"

"I'm on the edge of my seat." She made a show of settling even deeper into the cozy couch that felt like a giant hug.

"It's all about warming the flue." Striking a match, he lit the last ball of newspaper. Then he held the match over the logs in the fireplace. "Like so. A warmed flue coaxes smoke up the chimney, so that it doesn't blow the other way and fill the house."

"Fascinating." She raised an eyebrow. "You're telling me this *why?*"

He dropped the flaming newspaper just before it singed his fingers. Then he used another match to light the other bits of newspaper. "Seems like you live in a smoky house, that's all. Clear it out and you'll breathe easier and see better."

"Thanks, Confucius. I'll have to ponder that. For the moment I just want to get through the pageant and then focus on expanding my kennel."

Sullivan winced. "You really want to add more coyotes?"

"I really want to save more dogs. Dorset Hills has a no-kill policy, so they ship strays and surrendered dogs off to other towns that don't. Out of sight, out of mind."

"What?" He turned to stare at her. "I didn't know that."

"Most people don't. It doesn't fit with the Dog Town brand."

"Huh." Using an iron poker, he adjusted a log. "What a shame."

"If I manage to get a kennel license, I can save a few more each year. But the dog cop told me three strikes and I'm out." Staring at the now-roaring fire, she sighed. "Twelve years in my old place without a single complaint and now two in the same month."

"I guess it's too late to install soundproofing, although that would go a long way."

"In the short term there has to be an easier—and cheaper—way."

He set a screen over the open fire. "Maybe it's time to deliver some home-baked cookies to the neighbors."

"You think I have time for baking?"

He perched beside her on the couch. "I think you have time to buy some nice cookies and put them on one of your plates. And when people deliver it back, you invite them in. Be neighborly. Show them you're not scary."

"Scary! I'm not scary." Her voice rose a notch and Beau moved to keep an eye on Sullivan.

"You kinda are." He jabbed a thumb in Beau's direction. "And he's scarier."

"I'm only scary to people who are trying to wreck this town's character and put up high-rises."

Picking up a magazine from the oak coffee table, Sullivan fluttered its pages. "You don't know me, or my work."

"I know you rode into town on a bulldozer. That's enough."

He snorted. "Good one. You also know the population in Dorset Hills has spiked in the past few years. In your view, where should these people live? Tent villages in the hills?"

"The City shouldn't let more people in than we can comfortably accommodate."

"The people we elect make decisions about who moves here. All I can do is build places they can live that still honor the landscape and history. If you looked at some of my designs, maybe you wouldn't be so prejudiced."

"I'm not prejudiced."

"You're one of the most prejudiced people I've had the dubious pleasure of meeting in Dog Town."

Bridget got to her feet. "I really appreciate this lesson on how to be neighborly, Sullivan. Guess I've got some work ahead to live up to your example."

He followed her to the door, smirking. "Did you hear that, Beau? The sound of your owner's mind snapping shut."

"Did you hear *that*, Beau?" she countered. "The sound of a pot calling a kettle black."

Sullivan shoved his bare feet into already-laced sneakers and grabbed his leather jacket. He pulled keys out of the pocket and jingled them. "Let's go."

"If you're offering a ride, thanks, but I can walk."

Opening the door, he held it for her. "This is what being neighborly looks like, Bridget. I saw the dirt on your knees. You fell on your way over."

"I'll take the road back."

"How about you take the ride that's offered? If you feel like delivering some store-bought cookies on a china plate to thank me, I'll return it happily."

"Do I look like I own china?" she grumbled, walking behind him. "And what's with this car, anyway? It's too small to be functional."

Shaking his head, he opened the passenger door, and flipped a lever to move the front seat forward. Then he stood back as Bridget coaxed Beau to get in. The dog dug in his paws and refused to budge. Finally, she had to half-lift, half-shove him into the back.

When she finally turned, she was out of breath, and Sullivan was grinning. "I enjoyed that. Thank you. I'll let you off the hook on the cookies."

"Like that was going to happen anyway." She slid into the low front seat, and Beau stuck his head in between them.

"Do you mind?" Sullivan said, raising an elbow to ease Beau back. "I'll do the driving."

"If you ever want a dog, I advise against genuine leather seats," Bridget said. "Mind you, the only dog that'd fit comfortably in here is a Chihuahua."

"I like small dogs," he said. "I'm not the one who's prejudiced."

"Fine. If I rescue one, I'll keep you in mind."

He patted the left side of his chest. "Perfect. There's just enough room in here for that."

CHAPTER SIXTEEN

"It's about time," Frank said, when Bridget came into Bone Appetit just before noon. "You're late."

"Cut me some slack, boss" she said. "I've been running around all morning delivering cookies and being nice to my neighbors—knowing at least one of them called the CCD on my dogs. Can you imagine how draining that was?"

"You poor thing," Rachel said. "You look like you could use a hug."

"I'll pass," Bridget said, smiling to soften the blow. "Several complete strangers hugged me this morning. You'd think they'd never had a store-bought cookie before."

"That kind of gesture never gets stale," Rachel said. "I bet it'll do a world of good."

Bridget hung her coat on a hook and took the apron Frank offered. "I can't wait till the pageant's over and I can go back to being a bitch."

"Won't happen," he said. "The problem with being nice is that your tips go up and it becomes self-perpetuating."

"You were never that, anyway," Rachel said, handing her the coffee pot. "Just a little crusty."

Bridget did her rounds, calming quickly as she filled cups and exchanged pleasantries. When all her regulars were there, she felt anchored in the world.

Half an hour into her shift, the entire Rescue Mafia came in. "All of you?" Frank asked. "Don't you people have jobs?"

"Oh, Frank, do I have to teach you how to be nice?" Bridget asked. "Maybe I'll offer a course."

Maisie and Nika delivered a kiss on each of Frank's cheeks, and he actually blushed.

"I only meant that Bridget is working right now," he said. "And she works harder when you're not distracting her."

"Are people complaining?" Bridget said, more to her customers than Frank.

"Not me," said Trent, the retired cop, nursing his coffee. "We're not complaining about Bridget's backup singers, so why should you?"

"No complaints here," one of the firefighters said, as she delivered brimming all-day breakfast plates. They were so predictable: if they were in before two, they had breakfast. After two, burgers.

On the way back to the counter, she dropped another glass of pencil crayons off with Gerry. As always, he was quietly coloring his favorite breeds. "Why never a Rottweiler, Gerry?" she asked, just to be pleasant.

"They're vicious," he said. "A pink and purple cairn terrier would never bite."

"I agree," Bridget said, laughing. It was the first time she'd know him to be intentionally funny.

When she got back to the counter, Cori, Maisie, Nika and Duff had lined up on the stools. Frank set cups in front of each one and poured coffee. "On the house," he said. "As usual."

"Just as it should be," Bridget said, "because what you've got here is counter candy."

"I'd get sued for saying something like that," Frank said, grinning. "Anyway, nothing personal, ladies. You know I like you."

"We do, Frank," Duff said. "And you're not completely wrong. We all chose flexible jobs on purpose so that we could drop everything to come and harass you."

"Harass us instead," one of the firefighters called.

"Settle, boys," Bridget called back. "We've got important rescue business to discuss."

"Heard about the noise complaint," Trent said, shaking his head. "That dog cop has a Napoleon complex."

"You heard already? It was only last night."

"That's a year in Dog Town time."

Bridget twisted her hair into a ponytail. "I'd hoped to get to the sponsors before they heard."

"You'd need a time machine," Trent said. "Better start damage control."

"That's what we're here for," Cori said. "Let's get to work."

"Bridget?" The small voice belonged to Grace.

"More hot water. Right. Coming, Grace." She filled a teapot and exchanged it with the one on Grace's table.

"Are your dogs okay?" Grace asked, taking the sugar substitute out of her purse. Bridget noticed she had an entire bottle of fat-free salad dressing in there today.

"I guess. Something's clearly got them on edge, but I have no idea what it is. Sullivan suggested soundproofing."

Grace tapped a few white crystals into pale tea. "Good idea. He's so smart."

"He is that," Bridget grudgingly admitted, before heading back to the counter.

Cori took over from there. "Let's go over the options. We could farm out the dogs, and get them all upset just days before the pageant."

Bridget shook her head. "They'll misbehave at the event and have trouble settling in their new homes. Bad for the dogs, bad for my rep."

Duff pitched next. "We could make sure someone is there with them 24-7. It's tricky, considering *that we do work, Frank.*"

"Not real jobs," Frank said. "All you care about is dogs."

"What else is there?" Nika said, batting her eyelashes.

"Ladies. Focus," Cori said. "Consistency is the most important thing for dogs. They thrive on routine."

"Full-time babysitting might not be enough, anyway," Bridget said. "The dogs were spooked last night. Even Beau was restless and pacing."

"Weird," Cori said. "Have you seen any wildlife?"

Bridget shook her head. "But I can't help thinking something's creeping around. Soundproofing would help keep noise out as well as in."

"It's an old house," Duff said. "Impossible to do a reno like that on the fly."

"How about using the barn?" Nika suggested. "Just portion off a room and slap up layers of soundproofing. Then toss in a bunch of dog beds and even a TV for ambient noise."

"That's not a bad idea," Cori said. "We train the dogs in there all the time, so they're comfortable with it."

"How would I get someone in fast enough to do that? Let alone afford it."

"I know a guy," Trent said, picking up his phone. "New

in town and looking for work. Did a great job repairing my garage."

"I don't have the money, Trent."

"Leap and the net shall appear," he said.

Bridget scowled at him. "What does that mean?"

"It means things will work out, honey," Rachel said, patting her shoulder. "Trust the universe."

Cori snorted. "The universe has been in a foul mood lately."

Trent got up and came over to the counter. "You're on for tomorrow. He's bringing some friends so it can be done in a day."

"I'll help," said Rod, one of the firefighters. "We're off duty."

"Count me in," another one said.

"Guys, seriously, you're amazing." Bridget's eyes filled with tears.

"She's crying," Frank said. "Has hell frozen over?"

"Now, stop it," Rachel said, looking at him pointedly. "What she needs is money."

"Oh, no. Not another advance." He backed away with his hands raised.

"Just give her the money." Rachel wagged her finger at him. "One day you're going to realize you want her to take over the place so that you can sit in a booth and yell at us. You might as well start laying the groundwork."

"Take over?" Frank looked baffled.

"Frank, we're no spring chickens, you and me. Time to start succession planning."

"Rachel, don't," Bridget said. "Frank's going to be bossing us around a long time yet. At least, I hope so."

The door opened and a cool breeze blew through the place. Sullivan Shaw stood in the doorway. The counter candy spun on their stools for a better look. Meanwhile, Grace waved eagerly from her table.

Sullivan waved to Grace, but he came directly to the counter. "Thanks for the cookies, Bridget. What a sweet surprise."

All heads turned to Bridget. And back to Sullivan. And back to Bridget. By which point, her cheeks had practically detonated. "It was smoky," she said. "Thought I'd warm up the flue."

He laughed. "Quick study. Impressive."

"Was that a secret language?" Cori asked.

Trent offered Sullivan his hand and introduced himself. "We're soundproofing Bridget's barn tomorrow morning. Want to help?"

Sullivan flashed her a grin. "I could spare some time for a good neighbor."

Grace's gentle voice called his name and he turned to join her. All the girls, and even the men, watched him go. There's was something magnetic about him, Bridget saw. At least she wasn't the only one who thought so.

When Grace called for another pot of hot water, this time Bridget pretended not to hear. Instead, she followed Frank into the back room.

"Look, I'm sorry Rachel was so pushy on my behalf," she said.

He sat down at his desk and sighed. "She's not wrong. One day I'll want to scale back, at least. And you're the obvious choice to take over for me."

"Frank, it's way too soon to talk like that."

He shrugged. "At any rate, I've been meaning to tell you that I'm proud of you. It's good to see you settling down."

"Settling down?"

"The house. The guy out there with his eye on you."

"Frank, that's—"

"It all goes so fast, Bridget. I hate to see you scrambling all the time."

"I'm okay, Frank, really."

Pulling his check book out of a drawer, he started filling it out. "I'm doing this the old-fashioned way. And you're going to cash this and give me a charitable receipt, for when you file my taxes."

Bridget stared at it, eyes glistening. "Can I hug you now?"

"I thought you were hugged out," he said, getting to his feet.

"Only for strangers. Not family."

CHAPTER SEVENTEEN

It was just after sunrise when Bridget awoke to the roar of an engine in the distance. The dogs went crazy, barking and running around the house. They'd become trigger happy, which was the opposite of what they needed to be. With exactly a week to go before they appeared at the pageant and joined their new homes, she wanted to keep the atmosphere as calm as possible. Yet the roar sounded like it was getting closer.

Throwing on her jeans and a sweater, she ran to the door. Coming down the driveway was a yellow backhoe. And driving that backhoe was Sullivan Shaw. When he saw her on the porch, he let out a mighty "Yeehaw" and set the dogs off even more.

"What are you doing?" she called, as he maneuvered the machine in beside her car.

"I didn't have the bulldozer handy," he called back. "You know, the one you said I rode into town on."

"You're an idiot." She shook her head, and started laughing. "Honestly."

He hopped off the backhoe and came up the stairs. "Is

that any way to talk to a prince on a charger? You could at least offer coffee."

A prince? What did he mean by that? Her heart beat a little faster. But then she remembered "a" prince was different from "your" prince. In fact, he was Grace's prince, not hers. Even though Grace would surely not be as amused at his riding in on a backhoe as she was. The machine would rattle her china dolls on their shelves.

That said, Bridget's house was rattling, too. The dogs had become absolutely frantic. Beau was making a snarling noise she'd never heard.

"Okay, I'll make coffee, but you'd better stay outside." She paused with her hand on the door. "And don't dig anything up while I'm gone."

He slapped the side of the backhoe. "Can't promise anything. This thing is barely tame."

Bridget opened three cupboards before she found the coffee where it always was. Then she overfilled the pot and spilled water on the floor. Coffee granules crunched underfoot after she missed the filter. It seemed like the dogs weren't the only ones rattled.

While she fed the dogs, she pondered the last time she'd felt this way. It had been years, she guessed. She'd dated here and there, but no one had ever made her hands shake till the floor was dirty. She didn't like it. She didn't like it at all. The percolating feeling inside might put her off at a time she really couldn't afford to lose focus. Besides, hot and smart and funny as Sullivan Shaw might be, the jury was still out on his principles. He was full-on flirting with her while Grace was probably setting off for the bistro to work over a teabag. So, no, she would not percolate over Sullivan Shaw. He could wait outside alone until chaperones arrived.

She let the dogs out the back door into the fenced side yard, where they yelled some more and she shushed them. Finally, the backhoe started up again, and by the time she got back to the front porch, Sullivan had driven off to the barn.

By that point, other cars were approaching. Soon the driveway was full. Sullivan was back, and even though he'd been the last one informed about the project, he automatically took over as foreman. Everyone seemed happy to defer to him, even Trent, who was behind the whole scheme. He'd arrived with a contractor named Carver Black. He was the classic tall, dark and handsome type, made even more appealing by the toolbelt he was wearing. Nika and Maisie fluttered around him like pretty moths, helping to unload supplies from Trent's truck.

"Hang on, Bee," Duff said, holding her back from joining everyone at the barn. "Have you checked your phone today?"

Bridget shook her head and followed Duff inside the house. There were four emails from the sponsors City Hall had sent her way, and another from Dave at Build Right. Each had regretfully withdrawn support for the pageant.

"What? Why?" Bridget wailed.

"They're distancing themselves." Duff put on another pot of coffee. "I assume they don't want to back someone the CCD is targeting."

"We need that money to renovate Seaton Dog Park. We made a public commitment."

Duff pulled all the mugs out of the cupboard and set them on two trays. "We'll find more sponsors. These guys were in the mayor's back pocket, that's all."

"So now the mayor hates me again?"

"We don't know that. But we can infer from the withdrawal of his sponsors that City Hall's pretty chilly right now."

Dropping onto a kitchen chair, Bridget rubbed her forehead. "It's a smear campaign. Someone is setting me up."

She expected Duff to argue with her, but she didn't. "Maybe. But we're not out of options yet."

"It's only a few days."

"We work best under pressure, remember?"

The dogs swarmed around, licking Bridget's hands. "Not this much pressure."

Pulling cream out of the fridge, Duff added it to the tray. "I've already sent out a bunch of emails. I'm sure we'll be fine. Later, we'll call Mike, okay?"

"It's like whack-a-mole. We get one problem solved and another crops up."

Duff handed her a bag of sugar and the sugar bowl. "Fill that. Sounds like Sullivan likes things sweet."

Bridget got up and filled the bowl. "Well, Grace is pretty sweet, I guess. For someone who doesn't use sugar."

"He's sweet on you, Bridget. That's pretty obvious. Grace is just a friend."

Grabbing a handful of spoons from the drawer, Bridget dropped them onto the tray with a clatter. "I don't get the sense Grace knows that. It's not right."

"Let them work it out. You've got enough on your hands right now."

Picking up the tray, Bridget followed Duff out the door. She only lost one mug and two spoons on the way to the barn, and that was a small miracle, considering how slippery the path was now that Sullivan had widened it with his backhoe. He'd also cleared the brush all the way around the barn. It looked bare and violated.

"It'll grow back," Duff said, seeing her expression. "It's good to keep things clear."

"I told him not to plow anything," Bridget grumbled.

"Be nice," Duff reminded her. "This is like an old-fashioned barn raising. It's amazing."

More than a dozen people were already at work, pulling down old boards and carrying them out. Sullivan and Carver measured and discussed, and then discussed and measured again, before cutting the new wood. The preparation seemed arduous, but after a certain point, everything came together quickly. The hammering was loud and the laughter louder. Maisie worked alongside Ron, and it seemed like there was as much flirting as work going on.

Cori had moved up the ranks and assigned herself official crew leader. She was the only one whose vote vetoed Sullivan's. "No," she said, more than once. "The dogs wouldn't like that."

Sullivan and Carver exchanged glances but fell in line. The dogs were ultimately at the helm.

The room shaped up beautifully. It was 16 feet square, with layers of soundproofing. There were plenty of vents, and only a few long, high windows. The point was to build a spa retreat, and the dogs would never be in there for more than a few hours.

By noon, they were down to the final touches. "Let's get out the power sanders and smooth it all down," Carver said.

They carried in two sanders, and plugged them in. The roar was deafening, but only for a moment. Then there was an odd whooshing sound followed by silence.

"What the hell?" Carver said. "We blew the power."

"Doesn't make sense," Sullivan said. "The wiring's fine for that load. I had it inspected."

Carver gave him a strange look. "You had it inspected?"

Glancing at Bridget, Sullivan said, "Long story, but yes."

Ron's head was back and his nostrils flared. Then he shouted, "Fire."

The shout rippled through the barn. Everyone scrambled, looking for the source. In the opposite corner from the room they'd built, a few flames licked out from under the panelling. Someone brought in a hose and hooked it up while others grabbed drop cloths and soaked them. In short order, the fire was out.

"Way to ruin a good barn raising," Trent said.

Duff and Nika took Bridget's arms and led her outside. "I'm fine," she protested.

"You're as white as that drop sheet," Duff countered. "Just sit down a moment."

"I'm not—"

"Bridget, sit," Sullivan said, pointing to a massive toolbox near Carver's truck. "Just catch your breath, and we can sort this out."

Shaking off her friends' hands, Bridget did as she was told. Her mind was racing like a greyhound on a race course. Sullivan's deep voice was calming, even if he was giving orders like he owned the place. There was time to address his misconception later, when she wasn't worried about her house burning down.

Ron, Sullivan, Carver and Trent dispersed to examine the back of the barn.

"Stay," Sullivan said, wagging a finger at Bridget as he went around the corner.

Once they were gone, Bridget looked up at Duff. "I can't believe I almost fainted. It's so embarrassing."

"Bee, it's a totally normal reaction to seeing your house

on fire. Or your barn, for that matter. Plus, you've been under so much pressure. Just keep breathing, okay?"

"Sullivan was right. The inspection said the wiring in here was sound," Bridget said.

"It was and now it's not. Welcome to the uncertainties of home ownership." Duff patted her shoulder. "It's nothing an electrician can't fix."

"Bridget, come!" It was Sullivan's voice out behind the barn.

Duff laughed. "It's cute, how he speaks to you in a language you understand."

"It's annoying," Bridget said, leading Duff over the freshly dug-out soil to a corner at the rear of the barn. Ron and Sullivan were on one knee, while Carver and Trent leaned over them.

"What's going on?" Bridget asked.

"This board was loose," Ron said. "It came away too easily."

"Squirrels?" Trent asked.

Carver ran his fingers along the edge. "Not unless they know how to use a crowbar."

Bridget's heart raced. "Someone vandalized my barn?"

"Worse," Ron said, shining his flashlight inside. "Rigged the power to trip."

Sullivan peered inside. "The wires are cut."

"Cut? You must mean chewed." Bridget's head was spinning, trying to make sense of it all.

"Clean snip," Ron said. "It's deliberate."

Duff and Nika grabbed her arms in case she got faint again. "You mean someone *wanted* the barn to catch fire?" she asked.

"Looks that way," Ron said. "I'm sorry, Bridget. I'm going to have to call in the fire marshal. And the police."

Bridget closed her eyes. "I don't understand. Why would anyone do this? My dogs could have been... hurt."

"We *all* could have been hurt," Ron said. "Arson is no joke."

The rest of the afternoon passed in a blur. Most people hung around, following the police and the fire marshal. Duff eventually insisted Bridget sit down again on Sullivan's toolbox.

"No wonder the dogs have been freaking out," Bridget asked. "Someone's obviously been sneaking around."

"You know who first came to mind?" Cori asked.

"Daniel," Nika and Duff said, together.

"Exactly," Cori said. "But if we tell that to the cops, it might come out that we stole Geronimo."

"It's a risk Bridget needs to take," Duff said. "This is no joke. Whoever did this doesn't care if he hurts people or dogs."

"I'll tell them," Bridget said. "If Daniel did it, Tina may not be safe, either."

"Who else?" Duff said. "There's no way this is random."

"Someone had to know we were planning this build for today," Bridget said. "Why else target the barn?"

"Word gets around," Cori said. "The neighbors didn't want you expanding. This sent a message."

A crow cawed overhead and Bridget saw that five of the big black birds were sitting on a branch, seemingly watching. It was hard not to see it as an omen.

"The investigation will take forever," she said. "And there's no way the CCD will approve a kennel license until this is resolved."

They fell silent for a long moment. Finally Duff spoke. "I'm sure the cops will figure this out, Bee. In the meantime, please stay at my place. You're not safe here."

"I'm as safe as a woman with 13 dogs can be," she said. "No one will come near the house while they're in it."

Bridget stared around at her friends. Normally they all looked ready to burst into laughter. Now, Nika was crying, and Maisie paced as if she wanted to punch someone.

Cori's expression shocked Bridget the most. Her warrior eyes were soft with pity. Resting a hand lightly on Bridget's shoulder, she said, "Bee, you've got to rehome the dogs. You can risk your own safety if you like, but you can't do that to the dogs."

That was when the seriousness of the situation really sank in. "Right. Of course, you're right," she said.

"The police will get to the bottom of this," Duff said. "Don't worry."

Cori became the warrior again. "And if they don't, we'll do it ourselves."

CHAPTER EIGHTEEN

"Chin up, chest out," Duff said, as they marched into The Dog House Building Supplies the next afternoon.

"Really? Must we lead with the chest?" Bridget resented that Duff had made her change into another sweater at the coffee shop. A tighter sweater, naturally, and one of three Duff had brought along in full expectation that Bridget's outfit would disappoint. "We are brilliant, accomplished women."

"Women being the operative word. Two women in Dog Town's biggest independent hardware and building supply store. We need to play to our *visible* strengths first."

Bridget trailed after Duff up and down the aisles of tools. "I'm tired of playing. This game is hard."

The mafia had stayed the night, speculating on who might be behind the snipped wires. The police were convinced it was just a scare tactic to keep Bridget from building a kennel, and were focusing on the neighbors. Bridget thought they were probably right, but she'd found placements for all the dogs anyway.

"You're tired, period. And no wonder after what happened yesterday. I wish we could call off the pageant this year."

"No way." Bridget shook her head emphatically. "Even if the money weren't an issue, I wouldn't let whoever did this stop me. And I won't let them keep me out of my house, either."

"Understood." Duff grabbed a trowel off a peg board. "Then you'll need to dig deep, my friend. We've got to seduce a few sponsors today."

"I object to the term seduce." Bridget picked up a hammer from the opposite side of the aisle and waved it. "I have my limits."

Duff traded her trowel for a fly swatter. "Pack your old limits away. Today we forge new ones."

Dodging out of the way as Duff tried to swat her, Bridget smiled in spite of herself. "The pageant's always been hard work, but it used to be fun, too. Maybe I should pack it in and focus on running the bistro."

"You'll never give up on rescue." Duff continued up the aisle, heels clicking on the tile floor. "It's in your blood."

Four men turned at the sound of Duff's stilettos, and their faces lit up. "Can we help you, ladies?" one asked.

"Absolutely, gentlemen." Duff offered her brightest smile.

"You're in the market for flyswatters?" he asked, gesturing to the one in Duff's hand. "In November?"

"It's to keep the boys away. Thanksgiving brings them out in droves."

The men laughed and surrounded them, renewing their offers of help.

Duff introduced herself and then Bridget. "Which one of you gentlemen is in charge?"

A balding man with a salt-and-pepper beard tapped his nametag. "That would be me. I'm Sid."

"We come with a very special request, Sid. On Thanksgiving, my friend is holding an event to refurbish Seaton Dog Park. We'd like to request your backing."

"The pageant, right?" Sid leaned back against the counter and crossed his arms. "My nephew got one of those dogs a few years ago. Nice little mutt."

Duff's eyes lit up. "Then you understand what this event contributes to the community, and how it can benefit local business. We'll post signs around the park and feature your logo on all communications."

"I'd have to ask the owner," Sid said. "You're leaving it a little late."

Bridget stepped forward. "That's true, Sid. Things have changed this year and we're flying by the seat of our pants. I only firmed up the location a few days ago." She described the event, and then handed him a list of the supplies they'd need.

"Whoa," he said. "That's some list."

"Nothing terribly expensive," Bridget said.

Sid looked torn. "I can't promise anything, ladies. The owner gets hit up a lot—sports teams, playground builds, you name it."

"This is different," a male voice said, behind them. "It's not just another softball league. It's an opportunity to back a local legend."

Sullivan Shaw joined them, carrying several yards of corrugated silver tubing.

Bridget's face burned. "Legend?"

"Sullivan's right, Bridget," Duff said. "You're a Dog Town institution just as much as this store is. It's a great match."

Sid shrugged. "All I can do is make your pitch to the boss and tell him Sullivan's backing you. That means something around here."

"Wonderful, gentlemen, thanks." Duff reached for the business card Sid offered. "We'll send you an information package shortly."

Bridget walked ahead of Duff and Sullivan, feeling claustrophobic. Duff grabbed her sleeve before she could escape out the front door.

"That was so kind of Sullivan, wasn't it?" She elbowed Bridget. "Obviously your reference means something around here."

"Thank you," Bridget muttered.

Sullivan grinned at her. "That sounded like it cost you."

She sighed. "It's not personal. I just hate going around hat-in-hand. People used to come to me."

He grappled with his armful of silver tubing. "With the tides turning in Dog Town, we're all going to have to do things differently. There's no room for pride."

"There's always room for pride." Bridget's tone was clipped. "At least, I hope so."

Duff gave her another elbow jab. "Sullivan, it's been a tough morning dropping off the dogs, as you can imagine."

Bridget reached unconsciously for Beau's head but her hand dangled awkwardly. She'd reluctantly agreed to Duff's request to do the dog-and-pony show without the dog.

"Who got Fritz?" Sullivan asked. "My little buddy."

"He's still at my place with Cori. She'll take him home later."

"Let me have him." Sullivan fumbled with the silver tubing; it sprang out of his hands and clattered to the floor. "I'll take good care of him."

Bridget appraised him curiously. With the tubing coiled

around his feet, Sullivan looked like an ordinary human. His blue eyes had softened from sharp to entreating. For some reason, he really wanted Fritz.

"This dog is a challenge," she said. "And he's been the most unsettled by all the commotion. I think Cori's the best one to handle him."

"I can handle Fritz. You know he likes me."

"Of course. It's only a few days, Sullivan, but I'm warning you, it's hard not to get attached."

"I'm the king of detachment," he said. "I'll give him back on time and I won't even cry, I promise."

Bridget grinned. "Don't make promises you can't keep. I bet you'll bawl like a baby."

"Inside, maybe," he said, grinning back. "But I have a reputation to maintain."

"Sounds like it's agreed," Duff said, opening the door. "Now, don't trip over that snake, Sullivan."

BRIDGET TRAILED around outside with Beau and Fritz, reluctant to go inside even though it was chilly. She was down to two dogs, and soon only one. Her pack disappeared abruptly every Thanksgiving, but this loss was premature, and more bitter than sweet. All her little goodbye rituals would be forfeited. On Thanksgiving morning, she'd collect the billeted dogs and go straight to Seaton Park.

Her eyes blurred with tears, and initially she mistook Sullivan's car for two vehicles. There was no mistaking the purr of that little sportscar, however.

He climbed out and Fritz charged across the parking area to hurl himself into Sullivan's chest. "Hey, buddy," he said, letting Fritz bathe his face in excited licks.

"Don't let him jump," Bridget said. "He'll think he can do it to everyone, and some senior citizen will go down hard."

"Fine." He put the dog on the ground. "You don't give Fritzy enough credit. He's discriminating."

"I couldn't leave him with the Fergusons for this very reason. I gave them Lulu instead."

"The Fergusons next door? You mean they fell for the cookie ploy?"

Bridget couldn't help grinning. "I suppose so. We had a nice chat when I delivered the cookies, and they stayed for tea when they brought the plate back."

Starting a game of chase with Fritz, he called, "I'm pretty taken with myself right now."

"Don't get him too excited," she warned.

Ignoring her, he darted after Fritz. Bridget couldn't help smiling. There was something magical about seeing a grown man playing tag with a dog. Whatever cares Sullivan might have, they were forgotten in that moment. He was quick and agile, but Fritz was even more so. As Sullivan dodged to avoid the dog, Fritz jumped and caught the fabric of his pants. He was literally hanging off Sullivan's butt.

"Fritz, leave it!" she shouted.

Sullivan spun and the dog spun, too, paws splayed out.

"Off, off!" Sullivan yelled.

Fritz wasn't letting go. Like most terriers, when he caught what he wanted, he held on to the death.

"Sullivan. Just stand still." Bridget was shaking with laughter as she bent over, grabbed Fritz under her left arm and pried open his jaws with her right. The left pocket of Sullivan's designer jeans was punctured in several places. "Are you okay? He didn't break the skin, did he?"

Sullivan's face seemed flushed when he turned, but he

recovered easily. "I don't think so. And I won't ask you to check."

Bridget sat down on the porch stairs and laughed till her sides ached. "That was the funniest thing I have ever seen. If you could have seen your face..."

"Didn't do much for my pride," Sullivan said, sitting beside her. "But it's nice to see you laughing."

"Can you imagine if I'd left him with the Fergusons? James needs a hip replacement, and he's already worried about winter. The last thing he needs is a terrier grabbing his—"

"Point taken. I promise I won't play tag with him anymore. Once bitten, twice shy."

They laughed together this time, and Fritz pawed at Sullivan's leg, asking to be picked up. The ploy worked, and he curled into a ball in Sullivan's lap.

Bridget looked at them sideways. Was it possible she'd been wrong about Sullivan? And that Beau had been wrong about him, too? She had been quite certain Sullivan wasn't a dog person and that wasn't alterable, in her view. Yet here he was, stroking a naughty dog looking very contented indeed. It felt as if the porch stair under her shifted a little. If she'd been wrong about that, what else might she have been wrong about?

"You're shivering," Sullivan said.

"Am I?" She crossed her arms. "It's starting to feel like winter."

"Let me build you a fire," he said. "I noticed the Olsons left a nice woodpile. You know you have to maintain it, right? Rotate the wood so it can breathe and dry evenly."

"I'll add woodpile maintenance to the list."

Sullivan set Fritz on the ground and headed around the house before she could decline his offer. She got up and headed inside, with Beau leading the way. The dog's posture oozed disapproval. Fritz's undignified ways irked Beau.

Bridget curled up with Beau on her old, battered couch and wrapped herself in a blanket. She should have said no to Sullivan, but she was grateful for company tonight. It kept her from thinking about her billeted dogs, or the person who'd vandalized her barn.

Coming in with Fritz and a box full of logs and kindling, Sullivan crouched by the fireplace. He delivered a play by play as he set things up. "Are you listening? You need to know this, Bridget. It's not like living downtown. The power was out for three days last winter."

"I'm listening." She was trying to focus on his words but kept getting distracted by his movements as he deftly placed the logs and sticks. His hands were large, but they moved with precision. His back was broad and muscular under his fleece jacket.

As if picking up on her thoughts, he turned and smiled. "Come here and listen closer."

Sighing, she surrendered her blanket and knelt beside him. "What is it with men and their fires?"

"Primal, I guess. A roaring fire keeps predators away, and our loved ones safe."

Bridget listened to his guidelines on placement of kindling to allow enough air circulation. Then she sat on the floor and crossed her legs as he worked his magic with sheets of newspaper. When he was satisfied, he handed her a lighter. She reached toward a ball of crumpled newspaper and he guided her hand here and there. The flames were warm, but not warm enough to account for the heat travelling up her arm from where Sullivan's hand touched hers. Passing him the lighter, she said, "This is a bad idea."

"What is?" He turned and little flames danced in his pupils. Devil eyes, she thought. Tempting her.

"Leaving Fritz with you. As you saw, if you give him an inch, he takes a yard." She slid away from Sullivan across the hardwood. "And speaking of yards... yours isn't fenced so please don't let him off leash for even a second. You know he's inclined to bolt."

"I've owned a dog or two in my time and none perished before old age, Bridget. Anyway, he won't bolt from my place."

She smirked. "You think your man cave is enough to hold this dog?"

"Wait till he sees the dog-food commercials on my big-screen TV."

"He's going to come back stinking of beer and stogies, isn't he?"

"We're more about whiskey than beer, Fritz and I." Sullivan slid towards her. "You going to offer me a drink?"

"No whiskey," she said, sliding away.

"I'll take beer, then." He slid towards her again. "Or wine. Or cooking sherry, if that's all you've got."

"Like I cook."

Again she slid away; again he slid closer.

"You'll get splinters if you keep that up," he said.

"Wine it is," she said, getting to her feet.

He got up too, and followed her to the kitchen. "You should let me sponsor the pageant."

She looked up to find the doorway blocked by two dogs and one man. "No. That's not a good idea either. We're neighbors."

"So you'd turn down the Fergusons' money?"

"I would, actually." She twisted the cap off a red wine

and poured a couple of inches into two juice glasses. "It would feel like a conflict of interest."

Walking over to him, she offered a glass. He took it, but he didn't move out of the doorway.

"I guess it would be a conflict of interest for me, too." He stared at her for so long that she had to look up. "Because I'm interested."

"Don't say that." Bridget's voice was sharp and she gestured for him to back up.

He didn't back up. "Why not?"

"Do I really need to point out that you have a girlfriend?"

Now he leaned on the doorframe, getting comfortable. "Is that so? Have I met this lucky lady?"

"Grace seems very nice, and she's one of my best tippers."

"Ah." Sullivan grinned. "So it's losing tips that worries you. Money must be pretty tight."

"It is, actually. Let's go sit down and I'll tell you about my cash-flow issues."

He shook his head, continuing to block the door. His grin was dazzling.

She tried to push past and he let his free arm drop around her shoulders and pulled her towards him. She took a deep breath and regretted it. He smelled like soap and smoke, with the barest hint of damp dog—a known intoxicant for Bridget.

"Sullivan," she mumbled into his fleece jacket. "Move of your own volition, or I'll ask Beau to move you."

He practically shot out of the doorway. "That's not fair."

Beau was waiting behind him. Tail down. Staring. Sullivan's scent had the opposite effect on him.

"Let's talk about what's fair to Grace." Bridget walked to the couch and patted the space beside her to invite Beau up.

"Grace and I are just friends." He tried to sit down beside Bridget, but Beau squirmed onto the couch, curled up, and laid his muzzle on her leg. "Really, Beau?"

She stroked Beau's head. "I don't think Grace knows that. She lit up like City Hall at Christmas when you walked into the bistro the other day."

He sat down hard on the other end of the couch. "Grace and I talked about this when we met. I told her right away I wasn't interested in a relationship."

"Something must have been lost in translation. Although I hear you loud and clear."

He groaned. "Must you twist everything? I told *you* the exact opposite."

Staring at him, she said, "It sounds like a conflict of interest, all right."

Getting up, he jabbed the fire fiercely with an iron poker. Then he threw another log on. Once the flames were leaping merrily, he was ready for another round.

"Hold Beau's collar," he said, crossing back to the couch.

"Why?"

"Because first I'm going to lean over you, and then I'm going to kiss you. If the dog takes objection to that, he's positioned to do some serious and highly personal damage."

"I think he might," Bridget said.

"I think he won't." Sullivan's voice was a low growl. "He knows I mean business."

Bridget's heart was in her throat, wondering how exactly this would play out. She expected Beau to sit up, perhaps even snap. But as Sullivan put one hand on her shoulder and lifted her chin with the other, Beau didn't move. In fact, Bridget could swear the dog gave a resigned sigh. One of them certainly sighed but it may have been her, just as Sullivan's lips closed over hers.

After that, things got a bit muddled, but as far as she could tell, somewhere between the third and fourth kiss, Beau slithered off the couch and lay down at her feet. Sullivan moved into the spot Beau vacated, and for the first time in years, perhaps, Bridget stopped thinking about dogs at all.

CHAPTER NINETEEN

"You slept with Sullivan Shaw and I'm only hearing about it now?" Duff demanded.

Bridget had just come home after closing the bistro. She'd waited to tell Duff so that she could milk the moment for all it was worth. "Yep, I slept with Sullivan Shaw."

There was a pause as Duff assimilated this information. "Okay. And how was it?"

"Nice. Very nice. Toasty and warm."

"Toasty and warm? That's a mediocre rating for a night of passion, Bee."

She didn't have the heart to drag out the ruse. "Well, I'm overstating the case a little. I did sleep with Sullivan, but it was on the couch, fully clothed. In front of a roaring fire."

Duff laughed. "Well, that's progress. You actually fell asleep?"

"Snoring and drooling, I think. Hopefully, Sullivan didn't know that. I was facing the fire, and he was snoring, too."

Kissing Sullivan Shaw had actually been wonderful,

amazing, and every other superlative she could summon. But she had been so exhausted that she literally fell asleep sitting up, with her cheek against his chest. He'd eased her down, and pulled her in close, and they'd drifted off together, spooning.

"Then what happened?" Duff pressed.

Bridget walked into the kitchen and pulled a frozen dinner out of the freezer. "I got a few hours sleep. Watched the fire burn down. Had a beautiful dream about this place overrun with dogs."

"Heavenly," Duff said.

"It was, actually." She slashed the film on the frozen dinner and slid it into the microwave. "I didn't worry about break-ins or arson or sabotage."

"You felt safe with him. I love that."

"Yes. Until..."

"Until *what?*"

Watching the frozen dinner spin around, Bridget let the suspense build. "Until... I fell off the couch."

Duff gasped. "Seriously?"

"Seriously. And Sullivan didn't even notice."

"Oh, Bridget." There was clicking on the other end, as Duff paced over her hardwood floors. "Only you, my friend."

"Right? Since it was nearly time to get up anyway, I left for work early."

The clicking stopped. "Are you telling me you skulked out of your own house without waking Sullivan?"

"I had to open Boners this morning. And close tonight. Split shift."

Duff was filling in the blanks on her own. "You didn't shower or change, did you? You did a dose and dash."

The microwave beeped, and Bridget peeled back the

film on the little dish. "I was being a good host letting him sleep."

"Meaning Sullivan woke up alone with the embers of the fire he made for you."

"Not alone. Fritz was curled up in my spot before Beau and I left."

The clicking had started again, furiously. Bridget was in for it now.

"What were you thinking?" Duff said.

"I wasn't, really. I just wanted to—"

"Run. I get that. But why? Don't you like him?"

Stirring the food around with a fork, Bridget looked at the empty box to remind herself what it was. It wasn't very appetizing. "I like him well enough. But this business about Grace..."

"Oh, there's nothing going on with Grace, and I'm sure he told you that."

"He did. But—"

"You're just scared because it's been so long."

Bridget sniffed at the frozen dinner dubiously. "I don't fully trust the guy, Duff. You saw what he was like when I bought the house. There's another side to him."

"Then keep your eyes open. Observe. The truth always comes out." Duff's clicking slowed. "It doesn't mean you can't have fun, Bee. You deserve it."

"Maybe I do, but Beau doesn't like him."

There was a sound between a sigh and a chuckle at the other end of the phone. "I regard Beau's opinion highly, but is it possible he's biased in this instance?"

Opening the trash can, Bridget dumped the frozen dinner, uneaten. "Beau's never wrong about people. I trust him implicitly."

"So, he attacked Sullivan for spooning you all night?"

"Well, not exactly. But he kept watch by the fire."

"Ah. So, Beau is observing. He's giving Sullivan a chance. If something untoward happens, then you and the dog can snap your hearts shut again. Will it kill you?"

"It might."

"It won't. Do we need to talk about all my letdowns? Yet here I am, fully expecting a happily-ever-after moment."

Taking a bag of Golden Oreos from the cupboard, Bridget pulled out a cookie. She twisted the layers apart and popped the good side into her mouth. Beau was sitting at her feet, and since there were no other dogs around, she tossed the other half of the cookie to him. "Okay, Duff. You win. I'll observe."

"Text Sullivan when we're done here. Easy breezy. Just ask about Fritz."

Taking the cookies, Bridget went over to the couch. Sullivan had straightened it up and cleared the ashes out of the fireplace before he left. "Yes, boss."

They spent the next few minutes catching up on business. The Dog House had come through with sponsorship, and two other local shops had agreed as well. "I think we're in good shape now, Bee. You can sleep well tonight. You locked the doors, right?"

"Yep. I've got my fire extinguisher and a baseball bat. Beau and I will be fine. I worry about the other dogs, though."

"They're all in good hands. And I assume whoever doesn't want you starting a kennel will be satisfied they've scared the daylights out of you. Get your beauty sleep, okay? You're going to need it."

When the call ended, Bridget got up and checked the doors again. Her hand was still on the knob when the noise started. The sound was chilling—something between a howl and yodel. Beau stood perfectly still for a moment. Then he sat down, threw back his head and howled back.

Fritz. She was sure of it.

Grabbing her phone, she started to text Sullivan. But then the yodelling howl turned into savage barking and finally a terrible screech. Beau jumped at the door, whining and desperate to get out. "It's okay, boy, it's okay."

Bridget covered the short drive to Sullivan's in about three minutes. He was standing on the porch when she jumped out. Fritz was under Sullivan's right arm, squirming hard. Bridget gasped when she saw blood dripping from the dog and landing in a small puddle on the porch.

"Oh my goodness, what happened?"

"Fritz pulled the leash out of my hand and ran into the back. I guess he cornered something."

Bridget examined Fritz quickly and found the gash in his side. "It's going to need vet care, but it's not life threatening." She put him in a dog crate in the back of the van, away from Beau.

Worry and shame mingled on Sullivan's face. "I'm sorry, Bridget."

"It's okay. He'll be okay."

"I'm guessing it was a racoon. There was this horrible screeching."

"I know, I heard it. Not all of that noise was Fritz." She grabbed a flashlight. "Let's go look."

He took the light and led the way around the back of the house. There, lying on the lawn, was a large opossum. Its light fur was marked by blood.

"Oh no, how awful. Poor thing. Get a cardboard box, Sullivan."

"A box?"

"Well, you don't want to just carry him, do you?"

The concern on his face changed to confusion. "Carry him where?"

"To the wildlife center. He's injured."

Sullivan leaned over the stiff little body. "Bridget, this possum has already met its maker."

"That wound isn't bad enough and the possum is too big for Fritz to have shaken. I think it's just paralyzed with fear. That's what they do."

Sullivan shook his head uneasily, but then he went around the house and into the garage. Bridget followed and waited by the van. When he emerged, she laughed out loud. He was wearing a welding mask, and hockey gloves. Flipping up the mask, he said, "I can grab it by the tail, right? It won't break off or anything?"

"Just grab it with both hands and shove it in the box, Sullivan. Those gloves don't look dextrous.

He walked ahead of her muttering, *"Just grab the possum and shove it in the box, Sullivan..."*

But he did just that, and Bridget quickly closed the flaps. Then she used her car key to punch a couple of holes in the side.

Sullivan made a retching sound as he carried the box to the porch. "What is that stink?"

"They eject from their anal glands when attacked," she said. "Or so I read."

"Lovely. Now what?"

"You drive it to the wildlife center."

He stared at her. "That thing is not riding in my car."

"Well, I can't take it in the van with the dogs. And I've got to run Fritz to the all-night vet to get that wound cleaned and dressed. I don't imagine you want to deal with that."

"Better than chauffeuring that stinking possum around."

Bridget leaned on her van. "Sullivan, I warned you about Fritz. Stuff happens with dogs. But I don't want a dead possum on my conscience, and neither do you."

"You don't know my conscience," he said, popping the trunk of his car.

"That box isn't going to fit. Either you put it in a smaller box or keep it on the passenger seat."

There was a string of expletives as he tried to fit the large box in the car's tiny trunk. Bridget couldn't help grinning, so she covered her mouth. Sullivan raised his hand. "Not another word, Bridget."

She held back the laughter as Sullivan placed the box on the leather passenger seat of his car and closed the door. He got into the driver's seat without looking at her and started the car. The interior light was on as he drove off. It made his face look ghostly pale.

Getting into her van, she continued to grin. "Never a dull moment, is there Beau?"

IT WAS CLOSING in on two a.m. when Bridget turned into her driveway. The queue at the veterinary office had been unusually long, and Fritz's wound wasn't considered serious or urgent. In fact, the vet had said it would heal up nicely as long as she kept him in a cone for a couple of days. This wasn't ideal for the pageant. In fact, Fritz was quickly becoming the ugly step-sister she felt sheepish "awarding" to any of the participants. She'd have to offer a lot of disclaimers with this rogue terrier.

Beau began barking halfway down the drive. Bridget hit

the brakes and inched down the last twenty yards. At the bottom sat a white van. Its lights switched on suddenly, illuminating the entire parking area.

Bridget cursed quietly when she saw Officer Miller get out and stand beside an empty dog crate.

CHAPTER TWENTY

It was still dark on Sunday morning when Bridget squelched up the path and shone her flashlight on the slick, wet chow-chow. She could have waited in the car for the others but standing in the driving rain was more tolerable than sitting still. Her phone pinged repeatedly. She didn't bother checking. Her friends would respond to the 911; she had no doubt of that.

Duff was first to arrive, clomping toward her in bright yellow rain boots. Bridget couldn't remember the last time she'd seen Duff without heels. Like everything else, it felt wrong. "Hey," she said, shining the light on the ground for Duff. "Watch your step."

Pushing her hood back a little, Duff said, "I'd say the same to you, my friend. I hope you're not thinking about extracting Fritz."

"It would be impossible to get him out of animal services. It's a maximum security prison."

"Then why are we here?" Duff gestured to the bronze dog towering over them. "By definition, a meeting at the chow is about an urgent rescue."

The flashlight beam wobbled. "Well, I can't leave him there, either."

"We'll try diplomatic channels, Bee. We could have discussed that over coffee at Boners."

"I didn't want anyone to overhear." She looked up and let the rain fall directly into her eyes. "Besides, the rain suits my mood."

Car doors slammed, and Maisie and Nika called good morning to Cori. Then the swishing of Gore-Tex and splosh of boots was all they heard until the women entered the clearing.

Nika and Maisie gave Bridget a hug, but Cori was all business. "How did this dog cop justify seizing Fritz?"

"Someone had called to complain about the noise of an aggressive dog at Sullivan's and knew Fritz was staying there. The wildlife center confirmed the possum attack to the CCD, and that was cause to seize. The dog cop said he was a threat to public health."

"That's ridiculous," Cori said. "He's had all his shots. At worst, he's a risk to possums and garbage bins."

"Obviously someone is spying on both Sullivan and me, and ratting us out to the CCD. Probably the same person who cut my wires. I feel sick about it."

"Me too," Duff said. "Hopefully the police will be able to put the pieces together. In the meantime, we'll try to get Mike to reason with the CCD."

"Mike's gone over to the dark side. He won't do anything."

"I agree," Cori said. "We could at least discuss extracting Fritz."

Duff started to protest but Bridget raised a gloved hand. "Let's hear her out."

Pushing her hood back, Cori let the rain soak her fine, dark hair. "I have a guy."

Maisie swivelled. "You have a guy?"

Cori gave her a look, the effect of which was lost in the dim light. "I mean a man inside animal services. A friend of the mafia."

"Why haven't we heard this before?" Nika asked.

"Because he's a valuable asset. The kind you don't waste on just any rescue. He could lose his job for helping us."

"Then we can't risk it," Bridget said. "I won't do that."

"We need an above-board way of handling this," Duff said.

"I've already called Mike and he's not answering," Bridget said.

"Same here," Duff admitted. "But it's still early."

"We could go to the media," Nika said. "Seizing one of Bridget's prize dogs would look bad."

Duff shook her head. "Fritz is no angel. He attacked a possum and they're known for being docile."

"Media would cause blowback," Cori said, agreeing with Duff for once. "The mayor will shut down the pageant if there's negative press."

"I've got to do something," Bridget said. "I feel like I'm in the crosshairs."

She looked at Cori, hoping for answers, but Cori looked down. "Let's bide our time. There's too much riding on this to make any missteps."

Bridget wiped the rain out of her eyes and looked up at the chow. It was light enough now to show his regal muzzle. "Boost me up, you guys. I've always wanted to see what he sees."

"Bridget, don't. You'll break your neck," Duff said.

Nika unfurled her scarf and tossed it to Bridget. "Wipe him down first."

Maisie and Cori knelt so that Bridget could step onto their knees. She reached up to dry off the back of the chow and then pulled herself up, with a push from behind. Slapping the chow's shoulder, she said, "Good boy."

From the chow's back, she looked down the valley at the city nestled between the hills, warm with golden lights. But the hills behind the city were hulking and ominous, and she shivered as rain ran down the collar of her coat.

"What do you see?" Maisie called. Her turned-up face was like a drenched flower, with drooping golden petals of hair.

"Same old city, but it feels different now." She slid off the chow and the girls reached out to steady her. "This might be the last pageant."

"Don't say that," Nika and Maisy chorused.

"Just being realistic," Bridget said. "Times change."

"I doubt that will happen, but let's make this a great one, regardless," Duff said.

"Agreed. We'll focus on City Hall and sponsors today. Frank gave me a couple of days off for working the split shift yesterday."

"I borrowed a truck to collect some supplies," Cori said. "Ride with me, Bridget?"

"I'll come, too," Duff said.

"Two-seater," Cori said.

They slip-slid down the trail to the parking lot, catching each other again and again as mud filled the treads of their boots and they lost traction. Finally, Duff went down hard, cursing a blue streak. "This is what comes of not wearing heels," she said, as the others hoisted her to her feet.

"Make sure you change before we meet at City Hall," Bridget said. "Appearances count, Duff."

"Very funny." Duff's hood had blown back and her auburn hair puffed out with the dampness.

Bridget smirked. "All I'm saying is that this is survival of the fittest, and the fittest always have good hair."

Laughter rang out as they made their way to their cars. No matter how bleak everything seemed, they managed to find a bright spot. It was the mafia magic.

"YOU'RE sure you want to do this?" Bridget asked Cori.

They were sitting in a rental truck in darkness half a block from the Animal Services building. It was situated on the eastern edge of town, among warehouses and big box stores, so that residents wouldn't complain about barking.

"My guy inside offered to help," Cori said. "I didn't ask. In fact, I tried to talk him out of it."

"Why is he willing to jeopardize his job for Fritz?"

"He works here because he wants to help lost and abandoned animals. Now he's seeing the City of Dogs distancing itself from pets in real need." Cori took a swig of cold coffee and grimaced. "This is how revolutions begin."

"With a Fritz?"

"With a Fritz. An innocent victim of a political regime."

Bridget pulled off her balaclava, ran her fingers through her hair and put it back on. "I don't want to start a revolution. I just want my dog back."

Cori put the coffee cup in the holder. She was wearing black gloves, but the middle finger—her flipping finger—was neon orange. Ready to flout the establishment at the least provocation.

"Bee, you know you won't be able to keep Fritz after this," she said gently. "He'll need to go to a safe house outside of Dorset Hills, where he can't be recognized."

"Like witness protection."

"Exactly. And when the hubbub dies down, we'll make sure he's placed in a great home, I promise. The less you know, the better."

The clock on the dash seemed to advance slowly, but as midnight approached, time suddenly sped up. They both started breathing harder—Cori out of excitement, Bridget out of fear.

"So, when the lights flash twice, we go in the back door, find Fritz and get out in under five minutes," Bridget said.

Cori nodded. "My contact will shut down power from the front lobby and keep it that way for exactly five minutes." She grabbed Bridget's arm. "You're good with this?"

Bridget wasn't good with it at all. She'd rescued many dogs from neglectful or abusive situations, but never from the City that was supposed to celebrate all things canine. "Remember when we rescued Fritz?" she asked.

"How can I forget? Middle of February in a snow storm and that little guy was alone in a backyard with only a plastic planter for shelter. We turned his life around, Bee."

"And I'm not giving up on him now."

The numbers switched over to midnight, and precisely on cue, the lights in the Animal Services building switched off. They pulled down their balaclavas.

"Let's do this," Cori said, opening the door and swinging down from the truck.

Bridget did the same, and nearly jumped out of her skin when a voice came from the darkness. "Wait!"

Both women spun. Sullivan Shaw was standing behind them on the gravel shoulder.

"Get back in the truck, Bridget," Sullivan said.

"What are you doing here?"

"Saving you from doing something stupid."

Bridget and Cori looked at each other. "Duff."

"She figured you wouldn't leave this alone," he said. "Give me your balaclava. I'm going in with Cori. It's my fault this happened."

"It's not your fault. Just get in your car and go before you're seen with us."

"Let him do it, Bee," Cori said. "Give him your hat." When Bridget didn't move, she added. "I'll make sure he's okay."

She wasn't sure if Cori meant Sullivan or Fritz. "I want to do it myself."

"Get into the driver's seat and be ready to roll when we come out. *Now, Bridget.*"

When Cori used that tone, dogs were known to pee out of fear. Bridget pulled off the hat and threw it to Sullivan. "Be careful, both of you."

The two dark shapes, one tall, one tiny, raced through the parking lot and around the corner. Bridget circled the truck and clambered into the driver's seat. The minutes ticked by on the clock. Just as Bridget was starting to panic, they came back. Sullivan was cradling something in his arms.

Cori opened the door and practically catapulted into the passenger seat. Sullivan passed up the dog, and said, "Drive."

The big truck seemed to lumber on the getaway, but soon they were on the main thoroughfare. Fritz squirmed out of Cori's arms to climb onto Bridget's lap, his plastic cone battering the steering wheel.

"Easy, boy." He licked away the tears rolling off her chin. "You're going to have a great life, just like I promised."

———

BRIDGET EXPECTED Nika and Maisie to be waiting when she finally got home around three a.m. The person filling the open doorway was far larger. She sucked in a panicky breath before realizing it was Sullivan standing with Beau. Relief flooded through her in a rush that left her wobbly as she climbed out of her van. Sullivan ran down the stairs and caught her in his arms. She leaned into his chest for a few minutes, acutely aware of his hands sliding under her jacket and closing around her waist. He kissed the top of her head and worked his way to her hairline. It was delicate and exquisite, and she may never have moved if Beau hadn't goosed her derriere.

Jumping, she hit Sullivan in the chin, hard enough to hear his teeth clack together. "Oh, sorry," she said.

"Nothing a root canal can't fix," he said, hugging her harder.

She tried to relax, but once more, the long muzzle gave her a sharp poke. "Leave my butt alone," she said.

Sullivan's hands travelled down from her waist. "I don't think I can do that. In fact, I can pretty much guarantee that I won't." Holding her closer, he looked over her shoulder. "Look, Beau. We had a good talk earlier. You're going to stand down and let your lady leader relax. She's had a tough day."

"That she has." Bridget let Sullivan turn her and press

her against the van to limit Beau's access. "A tough month, actually."

"Fritz is all right?" When she nodded against his chest, he added, "I feel terrible. I promised you I'd keep him safe."

"Stuff happens," she mumbled into his soft plaid shirt. "All you can do is roll with it."

"Like rolling with a possum loose in my car, you mean?"

Bridget pulled away to stare at him. "It got out?"

"On the highway, when I was going a good eighty clicks. There was this ripping sound and suddenly it was climbing all over making these squeaking noises and reeking of sewage."

She pressed her hands against his chest so that she could see him better. "Then what happened?"

"Well, I screamed like a girl, if you must know. I hope you don't think less of me."

Grinning, she shook her head. "You were a hero. A knight in makeshift armor."

"And how I wished I had that welding mask when the possum crawled over my headrest before it settled under the driver's seat for the rest of the ride."

"Good grief. What then?"

"Well, the nice ladies at the wildlife center were very helpful. Once they stopped laughing, that is. The beast froze again under my seat so it was relatively easy to get him back into the box."

"Nice! It sounds like he'll be all right."

"They said so. I'm less sure about the car. I had it detailed today, but their detergent was no match for possum poop, it seems."

"I wish I'd been there to film it. That would have totally gone viral."

"Speaking of viral, I hope that thing didn't have diseases."

"Only if you ingest the feces, which I trust you did not."

He pushed himself out to arm's length. "Bridget, if you talk that way I will refuse to build you a fire."

"Oh, please." She snuggled into his chest again. "You already did. I can smell the smoke. And I bet you talked Beau through the whole thing."

She felt him smiling into her hair and knew it was true.

"Promise me you won't sneak out in the morning?" he said. "It's hard on a guy's ego when a girl leaves her own house to escape him."

"I trusted you enough to be alone in my house. Think of it that way."

"I didn't hear a promise. Don't make me squeeze it out of you."

"Hmmm. Sounds nice, actually." Her breathy purr startled her, and Beau tapped her side to let her know it startled him, too. "But okay, I promise."

And with that, Sullivan scooped her up and carried her up the stairs and into the house. Turning, he waited for Beau to enter, and then kicked the door closed behind them.

CHAPTER TWENTY-ONE

The Fergusons were Bridget's last stop on her rounds to visit the billeted dogs on Monday. It was nearly five. She'd had a later start to the day than she could really afford thanks to Sullivan, but the happy hormones filling her bloodstream made it worthwhile. Somehow, she'd managed to do a Seaton Park site visit with full Rescue Mafia attendance without spilling the beans. Of course, Duff was so angry over what had happened with Fritz that her romance antennae were temporarily disabled.

When Duff's name came up on her call display, she figured her friend had come back online. "Hey, boss," she said, putting the phone on hands-free. "Still speaking to me?"

"Always. Even if I'm mad as hell at you." Duff was nearly shouting. Bridget guessed she was driving with the window open. Which meant she was smoking. Which meant she was anxious.

"What's happened, Duff? I can tell something's up."

"For starters, Mike called. The City suspects you liberated Fritz, although they have no proof. Luckily they're keeping quiet because a successful break-in makes *them* look bad."

"Let's hope that investigation takes a while. We just need to get through three more days till the pageant."

"So much can happen in three days." Duff sounded exhausted. "Look, can you pull over for a sec?"

"Uh-oh."

"It's okay." There was the sound of Duff exhaling smoke out the window. "It'll be okay."

"You pull over too. It'll be easier to blow the smoke in the right direction."

Duff's laugh was stilted and odd.

"I take it you haven't made it to the Fergusons yet?" Duff asked, when both cars were idling on the shoulder.

"No, why? Is Lulu okay? Did Mr. Ferguson fall?"

"Lulu is fine. The Fergusons are fine. But they sold their house."

"Really? They didn't mention it was listed when I was there yesterday."

"It wasn't listed. Word got out today that they were selling and agents swarmed over to check the place out. But it had already sold. An offer they couldn't refuse, they said."

Bridget's stomach had twisted itself into a complicated knot. "Who bought it?"

"Sullivan Shaw."

"Sullivan? Impossible. I was with him till nearly noon."

Duff let that go. "The transaction occurred around one, they said."

"You mean he left my place and went over and made an offer on their house?"

"All I know is what they told me, Bee. They said he made an offer they couldn't refuse."

Rubbing her forehead with her left hand, she rested her right hand on Beau's shoulder. He moved to lay his muzzle across her leg. "Sullivan now owns the properties on either side of me."

"So it would seem, yes. I hoped he would have mentioned this to you himself."

Beau shifted under her hand, and she realized she was pinching him. "You would think so, especially considering what happened between us last night."

"Oh, Bee, I'm sorry. This sucks."

"I guess I should have observed a little longer before jumping in. He must be plotting to squeeze me out and plow everything down."

"He can't buy what's not for sale. Remember that."

"But if the pageant is a bust, the bank won't back my bridge loan, and I'll have no choice but to sell."

"He doesn't know that, Bee."

"Everyone knows everything in Dog Town. How did someone know about Fritz attacking the possum before I could even get home from the vet? How did you know about our plan to extract Fritz?"

"I didn't. You're just predictable."

"But now we know Sullivan's a sneak and a liar. Who's to say he isn't spreading the word about rescuing Fritz? Then City Hall will shut down the pageant and Sullivan can scoop my house right out from under me."

"He won't do that. He implicated himself in that rescue. Just stop for a moment and breathe. I know this looks bad on the surface, but you can't believe everything you see. Especially in Dog Town."

"Well, I'm about to find out, Duff. I'm driving over there right now."

For once Duff didn't try to stop her. "Call me after, okay?"

Bridget put the car in drive. "Of course. But chances are you'll hear all about it before I get a chance."

———

SULLIVAN OPENED the door as Bridget was getting ready to slam the knocker a third time.

"Hey," he said.

Just "hey." A guilty-sounding "hey" at that. And if a guilty hey weren't enough, he was shifting from one bare foot to another. His blue eyes danced around, refusing to meet hers.

"How'd your day go?" she asked, reaching down to touch Beau's head. Her hand landed on air. Beau was trotting toward the back of the house. "Beau, come," she said, and the dog turned back.

"It went well," Sullivan said. "I'm guessing you already heard what happened."

"It is Dog Town, so yes. I heard you made an offer the Fergusons couldn't refuse."

"I made a reasonable offer when—"

"When you heard from me that Mr. Ferguson was struggling with his hips, and scared about the winter. You rushed right over to push them out of their house."

"Excuse me?" He crossed his arms and planted his feet. "I did no such thing."

"So you didn't roll out of my bed this morning and rush over to buy them out."

"I went over this morning, but it's not at all what you think."

"Where there's smoke, there's fire, Sullivan."

Now his eyes met hers full on. He was as angry as she was.

"I can't believe you'd think that of me." His voice rose. "Especially when you took advantage of the Olsons by getting them to take a lowball offer from you out of pity."

It was like a kick in the stomach. "Pity? How dare you!"

"Why else would they turn down a better offer? They obviously felt bad for the lady who lived in the shoebox with so many dogs she didn't know what to do."

"They wanted their house to be loved, like a pet. And they didn't feel you could do that. Just like I didn't feel you could take care of a rescue dog properly."

He took a step backwards, as if her shot had landed. "Well, then. I don't think there's much left to say."

"Only this. Did you cut the wire in my barn? Because it's looking like the person trying to sabotage my home and my dogs and my future may have been you all along."

Anger rumbled in his throat like a growl. "That's ridiculous."

"Well, what else are you going to do with two properties and me in between?"

"I don't need to account for my plans. You're acting like the crazy dog lady I thought you were when we met."

"I thought you were a slick jerk, so I guess my first impression was right too."

They stared at each other and then Sullivan swallowed hard. "Look, this is stupid. Can we have a civilized discussion about this, Bridget?"

"No, we cannot." She reached down and again, Beau was not at her side. "Beau!"

Turning, she saw him coming out of the back yard. He seemed to be carrying himself awkwardly, but it was hard to tell with a black dog in the dark. She went towards him, her heart in her throat.

He barely reached the circle of light around the porch before collapsing onto his side. His legs twitched, and then his whole body convulsed. As Bridget fell to her knees beside him, his body stilled.

There was a terrible howling sound. It came not from Beau, but from Bridget.

POISON, the emergency vet said. They weren't sure what kind, or how much Beau had ingested. However, it was clear that if Sullivan hadn't driven her van so fast that it nearly blew apart, the dog would have been gone already, instead of clinging to life by a thread. Liver damage had begun and it was very difficult to reverse.

They'd asked Bridget all kinds of questions she couldn't answer. Beau had been fine and with her all day, except for the brief foray into Sullivan's yard. Few toxins could work so fast on a large dog. All they could do was treat the symptoms and send bloodwork to the lab.

Sullivan had offered to drive the sample to the lab, but Bridget asked him to go home and check his yard instead. "Just text me if you find anything," she said, refusing his offer of company. Then she refused offers from her friends, one by one. In this, the most horrible moment of her life, she wanted to be alone. No one could possibly understand what she was going through and making conversation was too much of an effort.

Her phone pinged over and over as she sat in the waiting room. Now and then she glanced at the bubbles on her screen asking her, "How is he?"

Only when Mike asked the same question did she bother to answer. With trembling fingers, she picked out the words: "I'm cautiously optimistic."

She wasn't optimistic at all, but she figured Mike was wondering if she'd be able to pull it together for the pageant in three days. She needed to put up a good front, in case a miracle happened and the show could go on.

As it turned out, Mike was assessing whether she was able to withstand more bad news.

"Bridget, I'm sorry to say the mayor has cancelled the pageant and the license for the work at Seaton Park," he wrote. "With all that's happened lately, he's concerned about the possibility of negative press."

She wasn't sure whether the mayor was bothered more by the CCD complaints, Fritz's rescue, or the fact that her home had been targeted by arson. There was plenty to choose from. That none of it had made the news was probably due to the hard work of City Hall's suppression machine. She wasn't the only one playing whack-a-mole.

Stretching out across several seats in the vet's waiting room, Bridget covered herself with her coat. Mike's news would no doubt hurt like hell later. For the moment, it was one less thing to worry about when she only cared about one thing. She could stand losing the event she'd put her heart into for ten years. She could stand losing the guy she had begun losing her heart to recently. She could even stand losing her house, which had already taken up room in her heart. All of that she could stand. But she could not stand it if the heart of her best friend stopped beating in the room next door. Without her big black dog, life would have no color. So, for now, all she could do was hope and endure.

It seemed like she'd only shut her eyes for a moment

when someone squeezed her shoulder. "No," she said. Tears seeped out as the truth flooded back into her awareness.

The hand squeezed harder. "Open your eyes, honey. It's morning."

Bridget's eyes popped open. "Mom?"

CHAPTER TWENTY-TWO

Bridget drank the coffee her mother handed her and slid down in the uncomfortable plastic chair. She was relieved to surrender the reins, although she felt sorry for the veterinary staff her mom was grilling. Bronwyn Linsmore, self-anointed dog guru, was totally in her element. By her own admission, Bronwyn had pretty much left Bridget to raise herself, but she'd always micromanaged her revolving pack of hounds. In that way, the apple didn't fall far from the tree. Otherwise, they had little in common. Bronwyn's hair was impeccably blonde, and her makeup on point despite a long drive through the night. Her attire could at best be described as bohemian. She wore floral print, harem-style pants, a sweater with pink tassels, a multicolored scarf looped around her neck, and an armful of bangles that jingled when she issued orders.

"What is taking so long with toxicology?" she asked Bridget, when harassing the staff failed. "Everything moves like molasses in Dorset Hills. It's one of many things I hated about this town."

"Some things move quickly," Bridget said. "Like information."

Bronwyn perched lightly on the seat beside Bridget, ready to fly into action as needed. "Andrea told me all about what's happened with your pageant. It's a crying shame, Bridget, but the game's not over yet."

"What can we do? The mayor has spoken."

"Bill Bradshaw? Please." Her mom dismissed him with a tinkling wave. "Bill hit on me at a party once, you know. Your father practically demanded a duel."

"Seriously? Mayor Bradshaw? Wow."

"He's not all that." Bronwyn looked around at the faces of other beleaguered pet owners and smiled. "I was a hot ticket then, my dear. Some think I still am."

"A hot ticket in crazy harem pants." A few pet owners smothered grins at this.

Bronwyn raised a finely penciled eyebrow. "I left in a hurry when Andrea called. It was a long drive, and I like to be comfortable."

"Well, thanks for coming. I wouldn't have asked."

"Trust me, I know that. I've barely heard from you in two years." Bronwyn unfurled her scarf and looped it more evenly. "Luckily you chose your friends well. At least, Andrea. That little bird Cori I'm not so sure about. Looks like she could peck your eyes out given half a chance."

Bridget would have laughed had her face not been paralyzed with grief. "Pretty much. But she's a loyal friend too, and they'd all be here if I'd let them. I just couldn't bear to have anyone around right now."

"I know, honey." She patted Bridget's leg with a jingle. "You've got an unnatural attachment to that animal that only a mother like me can understand. I raised you to love dogs more than people, I guess."

"I do love my friends, Mom. But Beau's special."

"He is that. Remember when I met him? He climbed onto me like a giant lapdog and went right to sleep. That dog has uncanny wisdom and terrific taste."

Bridget's eyes filled again as she whispered, "I think someone poisoned him."

"I doubt the poison was meant for Beau, hon. What type of monster would deliberately harm a dog?"

"People do. It's in the news all the time."

"Nutjobs like that would avoid Dog Town like the plague, wouldn't they? It seems more likely that Beau got into some rat poison, and we'll get to the bottom of it. In the meantime, I have the feeling he's going to be fine."

"The vets said—"

"I know what they said. When have you known me to be wrong?"

Often. Frequently. A lot. But Bridget didn't say it. "I hope you're right."

"I feel confident enough that I think you should drive over and check this Sullivan's yard yourself. I doubt he knows what to look for."

Bridget's throat tightened. "I won't leave Beau."

"Fine. I'll go crawl through this hottie's yard. Would that be better?"

"Oh my gosh, no!"

Bronwyn smirked. "Off you go then. I'll stay on top of things here, and call you the instant I hear anything."

Bridget only gave in because knowing absolutely what poison Beau had ingested might increase his chances of full recovery. Sullivan said he'd searched the yard carefully, but what if he'd missed the one thing that might kill a dog? If she hurried, she could be back in 90 minutes, tops. And despite any reservations she had about her mother, she knew Beau had a fierce advocate.

After parking at her house, she took the trail through the bush. Sullivan should be at work by now, but she wanted to avoid him if at all possible. In the daylight, it was an easy enough jog. When she got within sight of the house, she stopped. Sullivan's car was gone. Good.

Just as she was about to step into the open, however, she saw movement. Coming out of the back yard was a slim woman. Grace. Instead of her usual navy pea jacket, she was in a khaki windbreaker and chinos. If she hadn't moved, Bridget would have missed her.

Grace walked up the stairs to the porch and let herself into the house. A few minutes later, she came out, took a last look around and walked up the driveway. She passed quite close to Bridget, who was crouched behind a huge oak, without noticing.

When the sound of crunching gravel faded, Bridget sat down hard on the cold earth. Grace had a key to Sullivan's house, so he'd obviously lied about their relationship. And he'd probably lied to Grace about their relationship, such as it was. Maybe he'd only seduced her to get an in for his Wychwood Grove housing development. Or maybe he'd wanted revenge for her scooping her house from under him. Surely it wasn't because she'd denied him a rescue dog?

Tears ran down her face and she rubbed them away with the rough sleeve of her wool sweater. It shouldn't matter that much. Their connection had been little more than a week. They'd barely had time to warm the flue, so it was no surprise smoke was blowing back at her.

Well, she couldn't just sit there on the knobby roots of the old oak. Her best friend—a true, faithful friend—was hanging by a thread. If there was a clue to his illness in Sullivan's yard, she would find it. And if Grace or Sullivan happened to see her rooting around back there, to hell with them.

She strode into the yard with her head up, and scoured every inch of the dull, brown grass, and even into the bush beyond. She found a trail at the back that she was tempted to follow, but Beau hadn't been gone very long the night before. Otherwise, there was nothing suspicious around. It would have had to be something fairly tasty for Beau to bother. He wasn't the kind of dog to nibble on dead things. At least, not normally.

Finally, she peered around the far corner of the house. Sullivan had cleared a wide swath between the wall and the dense bush with his backhoe. There was an impressive woodpile at least five yards long, and the prints in the soil showed he'd been maintaining it diligently. Further past that was a brown compost bin that blended into the bush so well she nearly missed it.

There were prints around the bin, as well—human and animal. Judging by the dried claw marks on the plastic, the possum had been visiting, and likely racoons, too. On the far side of the bin was an old corn cob and husks from various fruits. Scattered on the dirt were shells of various nuts, and even chicken bones. Any of those could harm a dog's GI tract, but none was likely to cause swift liver damage. Holding her breath, Bridget lifted the lid and peered inside. It was full nearly to the brim with food that wasn't meant for compost. It stunk, but nowhere near how it would in warm weather.

First, she took photos of the bin and the ground with her phone. Then she pulled a spoon and a few baggies out of her pocket to collect samples from the bin and the refuse and soil behind it. She put them into her pocket, and then walked out of the yard with her head still held high. Good riddance to bad garbage.

Half an hour later, she found her mother holding court in the waiting room of the vet's office—not with the staff, but with the Rescue Mafia. They'd taken over a corner of the room and were drinking coffee from tall thermoses.

"Oh, Bridget, your friends are lovely," Bronwyn trilled.

"They are indeed." Bridget mustered a faint smile. "How's Beau?"

"The same. No worse, hon."

Bridget squeezed Duff's shoulder as she walked to the desk. The assistant took the samples from her and promised to send them to the lab immediately. Then she took Bridget into the back to visit Beau and left her alone. He was splayed out in a large crate, looking utterly pathetic. His lush black fur was already dull, and when she stroked it, it felt crunchy and dry. It was as if the essence had been sucked out of him.

Sitting beside him on the floor, she ran her fingers over his head and face. "Come on, buddy. Wherever you are, come back. I promise it will just be you and me from now on. Like it always was."

"Don't make promises you can't keep."

Bridget jumped. Her mother moved like a big cat when she wanted to and had long since mastered the art of deploying or silencing her bangles at will. "Jeez. Must you?"

"I must, yes." She eased herself down on the tile floor and crossed her floral-clad legs. "See what I mean about the harem pants? Built for comfort."

"Mom, I want to be alone."

"Well, that's not going to happen. You're surrounded by people who love you."

Bridget lifted one of Beau's feathery ears, grateful to find it still silky. "I just want Beau."

"Honey, I understand how you feel, I really do. A dog like this comes around only once in a lifetime for average people. Maybe two or three times for dog addicts like us. When Rexy passed, I was inconsolable. Between you and me, it hurt worse than losing your father."

"Mom! That's terrible."

"True, nevertheless. I could talk to your dad right up to the end, and we said all there was to be said. The break was painful, but clean. It was different with Rex. Excruciating. And you know, I haven't found his match yet. I figure it's a numbers game. I take in as many dogs as I can, and when I don't feel the magic, I find good homes for them."

"This isn't helping. You're saying Beau's my dog of a lifetime."

"I'm validating your feelings, but also making the point that you have human friends, too—a support system in tough times." She patted Beau herself, and the bangles barely tinkled. "Although I'm quite sure Beau is going to come around."

Bridget rolled her eyes. "And you're never wrong."

"Wrong is in the eye of the beholder, after all." Bronwyn grinned as she pushed herself up. "Thank goodness for yoga. Now, come out and listen to our plan to get the pageant back on track."

Bridget slumped down against the wall. "I don't care about the pageant anymore."

"You know what your father would say right now?" Bronwyn raised one arm and spun her hand so the bangles rang. "He'd say get up off that floor and kick Bill Bradshaw's arrogant ass."

"Oh, Mom, he would not." Bridget dropped Beau's ear, smoothed it, and got to her feet. "But that doesn't mean I shouldn't try."

CHAPTER TWENTY-THREE

Meadowvale Square was pretty in the summer, with its quaint shops and restaurants, and flowerboxes spilling over with color. On Wednesday morning, it was bleak. Frail, leafless trees along the sidewalk bent with the cold wind. In just a few weeks, fresh snow would fall and Christmas lights would add sparkle back to the city. For now, residents clung to their rain gear, still in denial about the call to parkas. But dogs had to be walked, so they gritted their teeth and got on with it.

The clouds didn't break as people gathered in the square around ten, but smiles passed from face to face like sunshine. Bridget was shocked to see how many of her clients and customers came out on very short notice. With Beau's condition unchanged, she had been sure she couldn't rally today. But the sight of so many supporters gathering to back the pageant soothed her wounded spirit.

Duff and the rest of the Rescue Mafia wove through the crowd, quietly sharing the details of the mission. Bronwyn stood with Bridget, resplendent in a gold faux-fur jacket and matching hat.

"You can't march in those shoes, Mom," Bridget said, shaking her head.

"I can, too, Mom," Bronwyn countered. "I've been marching in heels since long before you were born. Oh, how I love a good protest. People are too polite these days."

"City Hall hates things like this—anything that could bring bad press. It will probably backfire."

"We'll keep it short and civilized. The point is to be visible without being annoying. That's what Duff and the girls are telling folks. These people are hardly rabble-rousers."

Bridget watched Cori gesticulating as she talked to people and wondered if she was staying on script. The neon orange middle fingers on her gloves were flares in a sea of navy, black and gray.

The crowd was quiet as everyone set off from Meadow-vale Square. They were forty people strong, and many others joined along the way. Cori marched out front, directing traffic as well as the crowd with her flashing fingers. Then came Bridget, Bronwyn, Duff, Nika and Maisie. The route was simple, just a few short blocks.

Suddenly, Cori's gloved hand shot up. "Halt!" For a small woman, she had a good set of pipes. "And... right."

"Wait... what?" Bridget said. "What's she doing, Duff?"

"Going rogue," Duff said grimly. "What else is new?"

Cori stopped the crowd outside the Clarington Gallery of Modern Art. A surprisingly elegant bronze Afghan hound sat in the center of a drained fountain. Cori held traffic back as a pickup truck eased up onto the sidewalk. In the back was a fiberglass mutt of unknown heritage strapped down with bungee cords. Half a dozen people leaped forward and unloaded the mutt. Though awkward, it was easy to lift and place the mutt beside the Afghan hound. After some discussion, they maneuvered the mutt into a mount.

Phones waved as people captured the moment. Laughter rose on the cold air as the civilized crowd grew giddy.

"Oh no," Duff said. "City Hall will not like humping hounds at all."

Bridget shrugged. "Well, the damage is probably done already, right?"

Bronwyn was giggling. "Let them have fun if they can't have their pageant."

And so it went. The march that was meant to cover three blocks covered eight. All of the official bronze statues got company in the form of fibreglass knockoffs of mutts of all shapes and sizes. A long, low mutt teetered precariously on the back of the bronze Akita outside the Film Arts Center. Another mutt rolled onto its back under the bronze Belgian shepherd in the park across from the veteran's hospital. And at the fire station, Ron and his buddies came out and helped them place a huge shaggy-looking mutt in a headstand over their prize Dalmatian. The fire chief himself took photos, chuckling.

Bronwyn's raucous laugh soared with each new incident. "I was wrong about Dorset Hills, Bridget. I think I might even love this town."

Duff gave up trying to catch Cori and walked along, frowning. "Maybe I could enjoy this if it didn't threaten your house, Bridget."

Bronwyn turned quickly. "What do you mean, Andrea?"

Bridget flashed Duff a look, and her friend improvised. "The pageant is a major source of revenue for Bridget each year. We'll have to get creative after this."

As they marched down Main Street, Bridget did a double take outside the Dog Town Tavern. A broad-shouldered man had been standing in the laneway beside the tavern. Now he turned and moved down the ally with what seemed like a deliberately casual gait. She was quite sure, if he turned, she'd see the small cold eyes of Daniel Quinto. A shiver ran down her spine. If he was capable of abusing Geronimo, perhaps he'd found a way to poison Beau, too.

She thought about telling Duff about the sighting, but the crowd was already turning into Bellington Square, the large space outside City Hall. There, the frivolity fell away like autumn leaves, and the odd giggle was quickly shushed.

Mike was already standing outside, and the color in his cheeks suggested he'd been waiting a while. Bridget and Duff went forward to meet him.

"Ladies," he said. "I think you know where this is going. The mayor has declined to meet with you or reconsider his decision on the pageant."

"The people have spoken, Mike," Duff said. "They want their pageant."

"Their elected official has spoken, Andrea. He's offered a parade on Thanksgiving."

Bridget snorted. "He'll be riding a float surrounded by purebreds, I assume."

Mike almost smirked, but not quite. "I need to warn you, Bridget. He's received some photos and has officials checking to see if there's any legal recourse for vandalizing civic artifacts."

"There's not a scratch on anything," Bridget said. "We only disturbed the peace with laughter."

"You could use more of that around here," Bronwyn said, joining them. "City Council takes itself way too seriously."

"Mike, my mom, Bronwyn Linsmore."

Mike shook Bronwyn's hand—always a gentleman, even under pressure. "Bridget, the mayor sent me out with a special message. He said that if even one photo of the defiled sculptures gets out, you will never get approval for another public event."

"Did he really say 'defiled'?" Bronwyn asked. "That pompous—"

"Mom, please." Bridget stilled Bronwyn's jangling arm. "Mike, these photos are probably all over social media already. I can't control what people do with their phones."

"I'd ask them to remove them immediately," he said. "Because the mayor also advised the CCD to consider this strike three on your kennel permit request."

Duff's blue eyes welled up and spilled over, but Bridget's were dry. After what happened with Beau, it felt like a glass dome had slipped over her. Not much got in, and still less got out.

"Young man, you haven't heard the last of this," Bronwyn said, wagging her finger at Mike. Her coat sleeve gave a muffled tinkle.

Mike was looking at his phone. "I probably have, Mrs. Linsmore. I've been fired."

EVERY TABLE in Bone Appetit was full after the protest, and Bridget tied an apron over her coat to help serve. She wanted to get back to the veterinarian but couldn't leave Frank and Rachel struggling to keep up with the demand for hot chocolate her gathering had created.

The only table with a single customer was Grace's. She had come in for her house salad and tea before the crowd descended. Despite the hubbub around her, she looked as composed as ever. "What's going on?" she asked, as Bridget replaced her hot water.

"Just a few friends getting together."

"I heard about Beau," she said. "How awful, Bridget."

All Bridget could manage was a nod. Anger percolated up from her gut and threatened to spill out of her mouth, so she pressed her lips shut. If Sullivan had two-timed them, it wasn't Grace's fault. And if Grace had filled his compost with garbage that was unsafe for dogs, that wasn't a crime, either. She had no business being pissed at Grace, but she was anyway. How could she sit here stirring her insipid tea as if it were just another day?

Duff pulled Bridget over as she passed. "You won't believe this: we have a mystery offer from an angel investor. They're willing to back the whole pageant."

"It's no use. We couldn't get a site within city limits now." She glanced back at Grace. "Besides, it's probably Sullivan Shaw and I won't take a dime from that jerk."

"You can't afford to be proud, Bee," Duff said.

"Sure, she can." There was a jingle behind them. Bronwyn was wearing an apron and serving too. "My daughter can always afford to be proud. What she can't afford is to be stupid. So, why is this Sullivan offering free money?"

"Guilt," Bridget said, before giving her mom the broad brushstrokes of the story.

Duff silenced her with a finger to her lips, and a nod at the door. Sullivan had come in with a balding man who looked like he didn't get outside enough.

Bridget went behind the counter with intent to flee. Frank stopped her. "Oh no you don't. You can't bring in sixty customers—actual paying customers for a change—and hide out in the back."

Sullivan was already at the counter. "Can we talk?" he asked.

"No. Don't speak to me again unless you're pinned under a backhoe. And even then, I'd rather not."

"Uh-oh," his friend said. "The Sullivan Shaw charm has failed at last."

"Vito, shut it. Bridget, I'd like to introduce my college roommate, Vito Gardena. He's a television producer working out of New York. I asked him to drive down for Thanksgiving, because I think he can help you."

She took a deep breath. With Frank and her mom listening, and probably a dozen others, she had to be civil. "Hello, Vito. How can I help you help me?"

He laughed. "I like your spirit, Bridget. Here's the deal. I've heard enough from Sully about what's going down in Dog Town. I'd like to shoot a feature of your dog rescue pageant."

"Maybe Sullivan doesn't know that my pageant has been cancelled by the mayor, Vito. And my city rep has been fired, too. So there's nothing to see here, I'm afraid."

Vito gestured around the bistro. "Sure there is. We followed the protest, and now the community is gathered here in support of you. It's a great story with national appeal, I think. We could tell it one of two ways: Dog Town City Council rallies behind local rescue queen and puts on the best pageant ever. Or, City Council gets mud in its eye for quashing an event that's supported a ton of dogs in a dog-crazy town."

Duff started hopping up and down. "Oh my goodness, the mayor will freak."

"I hear he loves good publicity," Vito said. "Which angle do you think he'll buy?"

Bridget looked from Vito to Sullivan, and then down at the coffee pot in her hand. She wanted to decline the offer, and perhaps even hit Sullivan with something hard. Not a glass pot, but maybe a spatula. On the other hand, so many people had supported her not only today but for ten years. If she could bring some good from all this, she should probably get over herself.

Since she was slow getting to that point, Bronwyn gave her a little pinch. "Bridget. Honey. Remember what I said. Proud, not stupid."

"Thank you, Vito," Bridget said. "I hope you'll have more luck getting a meeting with the mayor than I did. But I'd love to see his face when you make your pitch."

Her phone rang and she pulled it out of her pocket. Seeing the veterinarian's number, she stepped into the back room.

"I have good news," he said. "Beau's sitting up and watching us work. It may just be me, but I think he's judging us."

Bridget sputtered out a laugh and a sob rolled into one. "That's my boy."

"We got the toxicology results back," he continued. "Beau had a buffet of poison in his system: raisins, macadamia nuts, and chocolate. But what nearly destroyed his liver was Xylitol."

"Xylitol?" It sounded familiar but she was too dazed to be sure. "That's rat poison, right?"

The image of Daniel Quinto came into her mind and she shuddered. It had to be him.

"Actually, no," the vet said. "Xylitol is a sugar substitute, commonly used in chewing gum or coffee sweetener. Do you know how he might have gotten into it?"

Bridget peered out the little window into the diner to see Grace sipping her tea and watching Sullivan.

"Yeah," she said. "Actually, I do."

CHAPTER TWENTY-FOUR

When Bridget walked into the mayor's waiting room that afternoon, she was glad she had taken the time to go home and shower. The matching love seats and armchairs were beautifully upholstered in cream fabric, and her jeans had been looking the worse for wear. She'd dug up a barely worn blue cashmere sweater and a black skirt with price tag still on it. Even her hair had cooperated.

"You look great." Duff actually said it, but Sullivan's eyes had said it first.

She hadn't made the effort for him, though. Or even for the mayor. Now that she didn't particularly need to worry about appearances, she found herself actually wanting to look nice. Duff had accused her once of hiding behind her dogs, her scruffiness, and even her Boners' apron. She was probably right, and it was time for that to end.

"May I have a word?" she asked Sullivan. "Outside?"

He rose and opened the heavy oak door for her. "Before you start, I need to explain something." Closing the door behind them, he leaned against it. "I went over to see the Fergusons that morning to offer to help them get ready for winter, that's all. They asked me if I wanted to buy their house. They said you told them I'd put in an offer on yours and they thought I might want it. I offered them a fair price, and that was that."

"And what are you going to do with two houses on either side of mine? I'm sandwiched by a developer. Imagine how that feels, when I want to build a kennel and stay forever."

"I have plans, but they don't include bulldozing your house, Bridget. Give me some credit."

He gave her a fierce stare and she met it with a fiercer one. "You're the last person I'd trust with my house and welfare."

"Excuse me? I just found a way to salvage your pageant and possibly bring in more money than you expected. Imagine how your pissing on that makes *me* feel."

Bridget poked him in the chest with an index finger. "Imagine how your girlfriend nearly killing my dog makes *me* feel."

"What?" He grabbed her hand and forced it down. "What are you talking about?"

She'd promised herself not to do this until after the meeting, but she couldn't stop. "I saw her, Sullivan. I saw her come out of your yard and your house. My dog is full of her poison." Blinking rapidly, she tried to hold back the tears. "I know you two don't know how to look after a dog, but seriously."

He dropped her hand and started pacing. "You saw Grace come out of my house?"

"Correction. I saw her use a key to go in and then come out. And your compost bin is full of her garbage. I feed Grace at the bistro nearly every day, so I know what she lives on."

"This isn't making any sense. I never gave Grace a key. She was only in my house once before we went to that wedding. Why on earth is she putting anything in my composter? I've never used it because it attracts vermin."

Bridget started pacing too, and they went in opposite directions. "Why should I believe you?"

"Because I've never lied to you, that's why. Grace is just someone I met on the road when she was walking her Chihuahua. She seemed normal enough, and I won't lie: making friends in Dorset Hills hasn't been easy. I thought towns like this were supposed to be friendly."

"You've got to worm your way in and it takes time," Bridget said. "Years, in my case. And look how quickly things can turn."

The door cracked open and Duff said, "We've been summoned."

They filed into the mayor's office. There were only two deep leather chairs opposite his desk, so Bridget motioned for Duff and Vito to sit down, while she stood beside Sullivan.

"Birdie. Hello," Mayor Bradshaw said, coming around to shake everyone's hand. He barely touched Bridget's and pumped Vito's longer than anyone else's.

"Mayor, you're a busy man, so I'll keep this short," Bridget said. "Vito is really excited at the opportunity to shoot a feature about Dorset Hills and my Thanksgiving Pageant. It's a fabulous opportunity to get some positive press for the City, don't you agree?"

"A feature?" the mayor said. "How can we be sure your story will be positive, Mr. Gardena?"

"There are no guarantees in life or television," Vito said, smiling. "But I have a vested interest in helping my old college roommate impress the woman he loves."

Bridget gasped. "Vito!"

"Just telling it like I see it," Vito said. "Sully's never asked a single favor all these years, and trust me, I owe him. So if he thinks your work merits profiling, I trust him. Besides, I've done some digging, and I can tell this story will tug a lot of heartstrings. Sounds like you're quite a matchmaker."

Duff's smile warmed the room and gave Bridget the courage to turn back to the mayor. "I do have some conditions, though, Mayor," she said.

His lips pressed together in a tight smile. "I don't think you're in a position to list conditions, Birdie."

"Bridget," Sullivan corrected him.

The mayor ignored him. "I could have you arrested for this morning's public disturbance."

"I got some great footage of the rally," Vito said. "I totally loved the political statement they were making with the dogs."

"Political statement?" The mayor's brow furrowed.

Vito laughed. "Well, the purebred elites were getting the worst of it with those fibreglass mutts, weren't they? A few residents told me mutts and rescues aren't necessarily welcome in Dog Town anymore. Is that true?"

"Of course not," the mayor said, rising. "All dogs are welcome in Dorset Hills. It's our brand."

"Whew! I was worried about that. It seems like such a nice place, so I'd hate to profile it otherwise."

Standing eye to eye with Bridget, the mayor said, "What are your conditions, Birdie?" He paused deliberately before adding, "I mean, Bridget."

"First, I'd like full control of my event at Seaton Park. It will show the very best of Dorset Hills, and we'll make sure the television feature tells that story."

"Fine. And...?"

"You need to rehire Mike, effective immediately. I simply can't do it without him."

"He's back in business. Are we done?"

"No. I need you to direct the police and the CCD to investigate a dog poisoning. I'm confident they'll find the evidence they need. I'm sure you don't want news of an attempted dog killing to get around."

The mayor's normally ruddy face actually paled. "Bridget, this is a very serious accusation to make in Dog Town."

Bridget took a deep breath and fought back tears. "I nearly lost my dog, sir. I have my theories and some evidence but I'll need expert help to get to the bottom of it."

"I'm fascinated to hear more," Vito said. "Let's go get some background shots."

Duff and Vito rose, and the mayor said, "I'll send investigators over immediately."

"We'll see you on Thanksgiving," Bridget said. "You'll be on stage with me, of course, and we'll talk to your staff about booking an interview with Vito."

"Looking forward to it, Mayor," Vito said, offering his hand. "You'll bring your dog, I hope?"

"Speaking of dogs, I have someplace to be," Bridget said.

The mayor's hand was still outstretched, waiting to shake Bridget's, when she left.

"I KNEW something was up the minute I saw that girl squeezing the life out of that teabag," Bronwyn said, as they stood on Sullivan's porch watching officers combing the property. "You could tell she wasn't a dog lover."

Sullivan raised his eyebrows. "Well, she did own a Chihuahua at one time."

"Which she surrendered. It's a sign of poor character."

"She also had a creepy doll collection," Bridget said. "I wouldn't disclose that if she hadn't tried to kill my dog. But I've never forgotten the feeling of all those eyes staring down at me from glass shelves. I never realized she'd moved to this area."

"The police think she wanted to live closer to Sullivan," Duff said, joining them. She'd been following the cops around, but the mud had caked up on her heels to the point where Dog Officer Moller had to set her feet free.

"You had no idea she was unbalanced, Sullivan?" Bronwyn asked.

He shook his head. "I barely knew her, ma'am. She was very quiet. But I had no reason to believe she would..."

"Go over the edge," Bronwyn supplied. "From what I can tell, this Grace had a vendetta against Bridget for turning her down for a rescue dog. She hung around the bistro watching for a chance to get revenge."

"That's how she heard about our plans to renovate the barn," Bridget said, shuddering. "Do you really think she meant to burn the place down?"

"I hope not," Bronwyn said. "I think she's just a very fragile girl. It was probably the last straw when you two started canoodling."

"Canoodling? Is that what we were doing?" Sullivan smiled for the first time since Bridget had confronted him with the news.

Bronwyn waved her bangles. "I don't need to know the details. But I can tell when my daughter likes someone almost as much as her dog."

"Mom, please." Bridget shook her head.

"Ma'am, I sincerely hope I can surpass the dog in her affections one day," Sullivan said.

"Oh, you poor boy," Bronwyn said. "If you think that can happen you're deluding yourself. You're best to aim for a very close second. It worked terrifically well for Bridget's dad and me for over thirty years."

"I'll take that under advisement," Sullivan said. "But I have to get Beau to like me first."

"Good luck with that," Bridget said. "Although you can start your campaign when he gets home tomorrow."

"On that I think he'll prevail," Bronwyn said. "Beau's a smart dog. I suspect he knew from the first time you two met that he had a rival."

"Mom!"

"Bridget, I just call it like I see it. Now, let's let Andrea order us all around so the pageant is a smashing success, and I can go home to my own dogs."

"I know they miss you," Bridget said, smirking.

"They do indeed. I've already skyped with them to tell them how much they'll love it down here in Dog Town."

She laughed and jingled into the house with Duff, leaving Sullivan and Bridget to circle each other for a moment before he finally went in for a hug. "This has been one hell of day," he said, into her hair. "Do you know what I need?"

"I do," she said. "I know exactly what you need. Let me show you my woodpile."

CHAPTER TWENTY-FIVE

I t was a classic Thanksgiving Day in Dorset Hills. The sky was bright blue, the sun shone, and the winds were kind. Somehow Seaton neighborhood had held onto its leaves better than most areas in town. Bridget almost suspected the City of tree doctoring. She was sure they'd all been bare the week before. But maybe it was just a change in her perspective.

There was no denying that Council had pulled out all the stops for the pageant. Mike and Duff worked together seamlessly, directing contractors with supplies, media and the TV crew, and volunteers to coordinate everything else. The mayor had even sent mobile grooming and spa teams to Bridget's house in the morning. The house had been full of preening women and dogs, and unlike her first makeover, Bridget had thoroughly enjoyed this one. Even Cori had succumbed, and she looked the spitting image of Audrey Hepburn. Bridget was a little startled by how stunning her friends looked, lined up for photos for the *Dorset Hills Expositor*. She had been seeing their hearts all these years without fully appreciating the packaging.

No one was happier about the free makeover than Bronwyn. She absolutely revelled in it, and when a stylist came over with outfits for her alone, she saw it as a bonus, not an insult. That was one of her mother's strengths, Bridget realized. She didn't get hung up on the small stuff. She was also a charmer when she chose to turn it on, and there was no stopping her on Thanksgiving Day. Everyone got a blast of Bronwyn's sunshine, even Mayor Bradshaw.

"Did you see that?" she said, coming over to Bridget, beaming. "Bill didn't have a clue who I was and he hit on me again. Twenty years later. I can't tell you how satisfying it was to leave him hanging again, Bridget. Upstairs, your dad is applauding." She pointed her hand skyward, but... no jingles. The stylist had convinced her to leave the bangles at home lest the noise interfere with the recording.

"Excellent, Mom. Can I ask you to keep up the good work? We need the mayor in good spirits and hopefully focused on you and not the TV crew."

Bronwyn took the job seriously and stuck by the mayor for the rest of the event. It gave her an excuse not to get her hands dirty in the Seaton Park build.

With nearly 200 people in attendance, including two dozen skilled tradespeople, the refurbishment didn't take long at all. The bare gravel was covered with a thick layer of fragrant cedar woodchips, and planters with trees and bushes sprang up all over. A team poured concrete in one corner to anchor the plastic agility equipment. The pond Bridget requested hadn't materialized, but the smallish fountain that did arrive would offer clean running water in warm weather. And unexpectedly, there was playground equipment for kids of the human variety.

"This is amazing," Cori said, joining Bridget. Her Audrey Hepburn glow had worn off, but she was all smiles.

"I'm going to offer free obedience and agility classes to get people more interested in working with their dogs."

"Sounds great," Bridget said. "I'll mention that when I announce the winners."

Throughout the build, she'd kept a close eye on all the pageant contestants. Two dozen people teamed up on one area of the park, laying an intricate stone path through some shrubs that would flower in spring. The project allowed Bridget to assess how well they collaborated. At this point, it was just a matter of choosing the kindest people and then comparing them with her list of the 11 remaining rescue dogs. She actually left the park for 20 minutes and sat on a bench across the street to think through the pairings. When she noticed the camera zooming in over the fence, she turned her back. This was where the magic happened. She had to feel it in her bones.

Finally, she was ready. She went up onto the makeshift stage they'd quickly erected and beckoned the mayor. Together, they called up the winners, one by one. The cheers, tears and applause made for great memories, and this year, great TV. Trixie Dayton was paired with Lulu, the dog the Fergusons had been caring for. Mrs. Ferguson was in tears, and Sullivan had to walk her out of the park for "air." Meanwhile, Vito swooped in to interview Trixie, and then Jonas Barnes, who had been unsuccessful in winning a rescue dog, but quite successful in impressing Trixie. If all went as Bridget hoped, that would be another match made in Dog Town.

All the pageant winners gathered with Cori and Maisie to get their instructions on care and handling. They'd be meeting for months, to ensure a smooth transition. It was part of the success of the program. And in fact, those sessions fostered the human matches. There was nothing like bringing like-minded dog lovers together.

"Time for the ball to end, Cinderella," Sullivan said.

Normally, Bridget stayed till the last person left the park, and then joined participants at a little after-party. This year, she left that to her crew, because she had a more important mission.

Slipping away with Sullivan, they drove to the vet's office to pick up Beau. Sullivan stayed outside to let Bridget have a private reunion. She sat on the floor and took the whining, writhing dog in her arms. The mascara so carefully applied earlier ran down her face and she didn't care. When she walked Beau out to the van, and got in beside Sullivan, she truly thought her heart would burst.

But the day had more to give yet. She arrived back at her house to find it filled with people and the smell of dinner cooking. Bronwyn, back in her harem pants, was at the stove, overseeing the reheating of a full turkey dinner, also compliments of the mayor.

"He's going all out for this TV feature," Bridget said, as she helped set the table with paper plates. She only had mismatched dishes for eight and they were already over that number.

"Honey, you need a nice set of dishes," Bronwyn said. "I'll bring a set down next month."

"Next month?" Bridget was craving some peace and quiet after all this hubbub—a chance to relax without a constant stream of people. It would be good to curl up before her own fire.

"I'll need to make it down before the snow, obviously." Bronwyn stirred the gravy and checked on the vegetables in the oven at the same time.

"You hate Dog Town at Christmas," Bridget said. "You said it's overdone and ridiculous."

"And I look forward to mocking it with all of you."

"It'll be great to have you back," Duff said, giving Bronwyn a one-armed hug as she reached for the cutlery. "I need help keeping the crew in line."

"You don't need help from anyone, Andrea," Bronwyn said. "You're a crackerjack event planner and you're wasted in real estate. Have you considered wedding planning?"

"She's right, Duff. You did an amazing job, especially considering the circumstances. I could never have gotten through this without you."

"Aw, thanks you two. I do like bossing people around! I can't do that enough in real estate, so maybe I'll plan my exit strategy in the new year."

Bridget ran her hand along the chipped laminate counter. "I'm sure happy you landed me this prize before discovering another calling. It's becoming Mafia headquarters."

Slipping upstairs to her bedroom, Bridget emailed her financial advisor to tell him the pageant had raised enough to cover the bridge loan, and she'd be in soon to sign the paperwork. He got back to her immediately, saying, "The loan's already been paid. I'm assuming you're acquainted with Bronwyn Linsmore?"

"Mom!" she ran back down the stairs.

"Don't run around like that, hon. You're flustering Beau."

Gritting her teeth, Bridget hugged her mother hard. "I just heard what you did at the bank. Why didn't you tell me?"

Bronwyn batted her eyelashes. "You need a fire under your butt to work that hard, Bee. I learned that long ago. So now, this is just a sweet surprise, and you can put the profits into building your kennel."

Bridget stood, slack-jawed, until her mother shoved her toward the living room to mingle with the guests.

Bronwyn's open invitation had been taken to heart. In addition to the Mafia, Sullivan and Vito, were Frank, Trent the retired cop, and Ron the firefighter.

There was a knock at the door and Bridget's stomach dropped when she saw Joe Moller standing on the porch. "What can I do for you, Dog Officer Moller?"

"For one thing you can stop calling me that, ma'am, as I am no longer with the CCD. I resigned yesterday, after getting accepted onto the Dorset Hills police force."

"Congratulations, Joe. So you stopped by to...?"

"To tell you the CCD discovered a footprint in the plowed soil behind your barn matching the ones at Mr. Shaw's composter. Also, several packs of chewing gum stashed in the barn."

"Chewing gum?"

"Xylitol, ma'am. Enough to kill a dozen dogs, easy."

Bridget leaned against the doorframe, her head spinning and her stomach now roiling. "Did you get her?"

"I'm not at liberty to say, ma'am." Then he shrugged. "Well, I'm technically between law enforcement jobs, so what the hell. Yeah, we did."

"Grace is under arrest?"

"Very much so."

Bridget pumped his hand. "Thank you. And Happy Thanksgiving, Joe."

She tried to close the door but he held it ajar. "Ma'am?"

"Dog Officer?"

"Right. Bridget. Well, Nika invited me here for dinner."

"She did?" Craning around, she saw Nika watching shyly from the kitchen. "She did."

"Only after she knew I quit the CCD. And that your kennel license has been approved."

Bridget grabbed him by the collar and pulled. "Get in here. And be nice to my friend, or else."

She closed the door and leaned against it, marvelling at the sight of so many people filling a home she didn't even imagine owning the previous Thanksgiving. At the stove, her mother was offering mashed potatoes off a spoon to Frank Mason. Bridget shuddered. No. That would be too close for comfort. They'd talk about that tomorrow.

Meanwhile, Sullivan sat on the floor beside the fireplace, alternately tending the fire and scratching Beau's stomach. The dog who never rolled for anyone but Bridget had his paws in the air, one hind leg kicking idly. They'd both been wrong about Sullivan, clearly. She'd have to monitor their biases going forward.

"How are you feeling?" Duff said, coming over to stand with her.

"Stunned. Queasy. But it'll pass, I guess." Filling her in on Joe's news, Bridget added, "I can only hope Grace will be locked up someplace were the tea is strong and the food fatty."

"I'm so glad this is over," Duff said, hugging her. "Time to look forward. And on that note, I take it all is well with Sullivan?"

Bridget nodded. "He's going to rent out the Fergusons' place to decent dog people so I won't have to worry."

"So, all's well in Dog Town tonight."

"There's just one more thing I'd wish for," Bridget said.

Someone pushed open the door, and Bridget moved out

of the way. Cori came in, clutching a writhing mass of terrier. "Happy Thanksgiving," she said, dropping the dog.

"Fritz!" Sullivan yelled. The scrappy brat hurled himself hard enough to knock Sullivan over. Beau gave Fritz a disdainful look and walked over to Bridget, who stroked his ears.

Bridget turned to Cori. "You'll work with Sullivan, right? He'll need a makeover to manage that dog."

"A trainer's work is never done." Cori smiled as she plucked off her gloves, starting with the orange middle finger.

"It's done for now," Bridget said, ushering her friends to the table. "Tonight, we give thanks. Tomorrow we find new ways to serve the good dogs of Dorset Hills."

I hope you enjoyed *A Match Made in Dog Town* as much as I enjoyed writing it. Come back soon and meet Mim Gardiner and lots of familiar faces in *Lost and Found in Dog Town*. Mim's mischievous mutt, George, has gone missing at Christmas. Is it a prank... or something more nefarious?

Please sign up for my author newsletter at **Sandyrideout.com** to receive the FREE prequel, *Ready or Not in Dog Town*, as well as *A Dog with Two Tales*, the prequel to the Bought-the-Farm series. You'll also get the latest news and far too many pet photos.

Before you move on to the next book, if you would be so kind as to leave a review of this one, that would be great. I appreciate the feedback and support. Reviews stoke the fires of my creativity!

Other Books by Sandy Rideout and Ellen Riggs

Dog Town Series:

- *Ready or Not in Dog Town* (The Beginning)
- *Bitter and Sweet in Dog Town* (Labor Day)
- *A Match Made in Dog Town* (Thanksgiving)
- *Lost and Found in Dog Town* (Christmas)
- *Calm and Bright in Dog Town* (Christmas)
- *Tried and True in Dog Town* (New Year's)
- *Yours and Mine in Dog Town* (Valentine's Day)
- *Nine Lives in Dog Town* (Easter)
- *Great and Small in Dog Town* (Memorial Day)
- *Bold and Blue in Dog Town* (Independence Day)
- *Better or Worse in Dog Town* (Labor Day)

Boxed Sets:

- *Mischief in Dog Town - Books 1-3*
- *Mischief in Dog Town - Books 4-7*

- *Mischief in Dog Town - Books 8-10*

Bought-the-Farm Cozy Mystery Series

- *A Dog with Two Tales (prequel)*
- *Dogcatcher in the Rye*
- *Dark Side of the Moo*
- *A Streak of Bad Cluck*
- *Till the Cat Lady Sings*
- *Alpaca Lies*
- *Twas the Bite Before Christmas*
- *Swine and Punishment*
- *Don't Rock the Goat*
- *Swan with the Wind*

Made in the USA
Middletown, DE
13 July 2021

44129464R00136